After a year's parting, physiotherapist Deborah Wyndham is at last on her way to Nigeria to join her fiancé Jim. But that special something seems to have gone out of their relationship, and kindly interference from the attractive Jean-Marc Roland makes things even more complicated . . .

NIGHT OF THE MOONFLOWER

BY
ANNE VINTON

MILLS & BOON LIMITED
London · Sydney · Toronto

First published in Great Britain 1975
by Mills & Boon Limited,
15–16 Brook's Mews,
London W1A 1DR

This edition 1981

© Anne Vinton 1975

Australian copyright 1981
Philippine copyright 1981

ISBN 0 263 73666 0

Set in Monophoto Plantin 10 on 10½ pt.

*Made and printed in Great Britain by
Richard Clay (The Chaucer Press) Ltd,
Bungay, Suffolk*

CHAPTER ONE

DEBORAH WYNDHAM came gaspingly out of a deep sleep, where some fiend had been striking her with horrifying regularity on the head with a heavy, blunt instrument, to find that the bad dream was born of the reality. She had, indeed, an excruciatingly painful head and her mouth felt dry and peculiar, as though it was lined with blotting paper. She made a few, unhappy noises and then heard her friend—and flatmate's—disgustingly healthy, bright and cheerful voice.

'Rise and shine! *Dieser ist der Tag*—or should that be *den Tag*?—I failed my German O level, as a matter of fact. Sit up, pretty one, and partake of the cup that cheers!'

The curtains were whisked aside and a thin November sun poured into the room.

'Must you?' asked Debbie, covering her eyes with a shudder.

'What?' demanded Elsa Lang. 'Are you objecting to my bringing you a cuppa? Perhaps you'd like champagne for breakfast, too?'

'Oh, no!' Debbie groaned again. 'It's the light, that's all. Oh, my poor head!'

'You sound like that old girl in the TV ad who has her aspirin brought by the waiter.' Elsa sat on the side of the bed and regarded her chum more closely. 'So you really have a hangover, eh? I'm not surprised. I never knew you drink so much before. In fact I didn't know you drank, period. Whenever we go out to dinner it takes you all your time to struggle through one glass of hock. You're only going to Nigeria, you know, for about six months, not to the moon. We do expect to see you again at Matthew's. Anyway, drink your tea.

It'll help. I'll bring you something for your head.'

Debbie swallowed the two tablets gratefully and gulped at the tea, which did help. She was able to think, now, reason and remember.

'Did I really drink an awful lot?' she wanted to know. 'I was nervous and tried not to show it.'

'Well, it wasn't really vintage stuff at your goodbye party, dear,' Elsa pondered, 'and your glass was filled about sixteen times by my reckoning—a good many times, towards the end of things, by Vic Marchant.'

Debbie flushed. 'Yes, I seem to remember him. Didn't he see me home?'

'How would *I* know, dear? I was in bed and asleep. At least I was asleep until I heard a car door slam and then the noise as it roared away. I had to leave my warm bed to let you in. You were quite giggly then, and said you couldn't find the keyhole and what had I done with it? So don't look to me for sympathy, young lady, this morning.'

'Oh, Elsa, don't be hard on me! I didn't mean to get sloshed, but I did have quite a lot on my mind. I still have.'

'But I thought you were excited about going to work in Nigeria for six months? You'll catch your plane this evening, and hey presto! you'll be in the tropics and with your darling Jim. After all, you *are* engaged to be married to him. Your late fellow workers at dear old Matthew's have had a whip-round and given you a super party, even if the champagne was made out of cider and soda-water, and I don't know what can still be on your mind apart from your last-minute packing. You've had all your jabs, haven't you?'

'Oh, Elsa, don't think I'm not grateful for your friendship and the party. It was a super party. Nobody was to know the honoured guest was absolutely terrified on two counts, and still is.'

'What are those, Debbie?' Elsa sounded really serious now. She saw her friend's pale gold cap of hair tumbled from an uneasy night and her brown chestnuts of eyes brooding darkly. 'You can tell me,' she added softly.

'Yes, I think I can. One—I'm terrified of flying and two—I seem to have forgotten Jim. I'm engaged to him, we have corresponded regularly, but it's been a year now since he went to be Surgical Officer at this bush hospital in Okusha, and though I can recall his face quite clearly, it's always as I saw him on the wards at Matthew's. I can't remember what we must have felt emotionally about each other. I—I can't even recall how it felt to be kissed by him. Also there's a third thing, though you might not consider it important. I do seem to remember telling somebody else all this last night, and it must have been Vic Marchant, and I definitely remember being kissed. It makes me hot to think about, because it was such a physical and temporal thing. That must have been Vic, too. I know I wasn't myself, but I feel ashamed just the same. I think Vic said he'd come and see me off at Gatwick and try to talk me out of going. Oh, Elsa, what shall I do?'

'Well!' Elsa had known Debbie for three years and they had shared this flat most amicably for two of them. Debbie was a physiotherapist at St Matthew's Hospital, in Willingham, and Elsa was a radiographer. The Jim they spoke of was Jim Brant, who had been a junior surgical officer at the same hospital until he had taken a course at the Tropical Surgery department of a London clinic and had then decided on the Nigerian appointment. Vic Marchant was one of the medical registrars at Matthew's, good-looking, a notorious flirt, but often excused his audacious behaviour because he was good at his job and always put his patients first and foremost.

Elsa, reddish hair buoyant and green eyes darting about the room, was obviously out of her depth for a moment after these revelations. She took the first and simplest subject first.

'I didn't know you were an aerophobe,' she said. 'You were all right that time we popped over to Paris in a crowd to the Motor Show. You enjoyed that. You've been to Spain and Majorca by plane. You had a holiday with Jim before he went off.'

'Yes, when I'm with somebody I'm not so bad, and I do remember that Jim is a very calm and reassuring person, but my stomach always cramps at the very thought of going up in a plane and I have this last-minute desire to run away. I may not let it show, but the fear's there. I'm faced with a solid seven-hour flight and I just know I'm going to be a wreck at the other end. I'll have died a thousand deaths just getting there.'

'Well, love, I can only give you practical advice. You mustn't let this thing get on top of you. I've heard of lots of people who hate it but have to fly for one reason or another. You either take a stiff whisky just before you're called, or a tranquilliser, but not both.'

'Oh, I don't want to be tranquillised,' said Debbie hastily. 'I want to be quite alert, just in case something's going to happen.'

'Nothing's going to happen,' Elsa said sharply. 'Statistics have proved that one's safer in the air than on the roads, nowadays.'

'And my other problems?' Debbie asked quietly.

Elsa looked as if she was thinking hard. 'Let's get number three out of the way,' she said dismissively. 'You don't really go for Vic Marchant's spiel, do you? I mean, last night he caught you in a weak moment and took advantage of you. No, don't look at me in that way! You know what I mean? You were looking for a shoulder to cry on, got a bit maudlin and found his. That's all it amounts to on your part, and he cashed in and did a bit of kissing. If he does turn up to see you off, and he must know you're not going to be stewed tonight, then you should be able to handle him. He may genuinely like you and think there's a hope of pinching you off Jim, seeing that he caught you in an undecided frame of mind, but that's something you must deal with yourself, isn't it?' Debbie nodded mutely.

'And about you and Jim,' Elsa went on, 'well, one does forget people and it *has* been a whole year. You'll probably just need to see his dear familiar face and all will return to you. I had a friend once in a similar position. Her fiancé had been doing eighteen months' research at an American university, and they planned to get married the moment he returned. Well, the wedding, reception, everything was laid on and then she came to see me saying she didn't know whether she even loved Brian any more. She couldn't feel a thing. I told her that was just too much work and excitement and that emotion did go on strike in certain circumstances. We all went to the wedding and they tootled off as happy as pie to honeymoon in Venice. They—that is—well, you see you're not the only one.'

Debbie knew her friend and had watched a whole range of emotions wash over her countenance towards the end of the narrative.

'And now?' she asked.

'Now what? Hadn't you better be getting up? I wonder if the toast's burning.'

'Elsa,' Debbie called sharply, 'burnt toast would have advertised itself before now. You're dodging the issue. Were Brian and this friend of yours happy?'

'Myra and Brian? I told you, they went off to Venice as happy as sandboys.'

'You're looking funny. Elsa, I *know* you. Answer me truthfully. Are they still happily married?'

'Well, it's odd you should ask that. It's ages since I saw them. They were very happy the last time I did.'

'Elsa! *Tell me the truth!*'

'Well, no, they've had a few trial separations. They're having one now. The only reason Brian comes back is to see the twins. But there's no reason why that should happen to you and Jim, Deb. I'm sure you're making more out of everything because you're suffering from cold feet today. *You* won't get married unless you're absolutely sure—I know that. But you have to go and see, don't you?'

'Yes, I do.'

'And it isn't as if poor Jim will have had much opportunity for emotional distraction in an African bush hospital, is it? I bet he's just dying to see you.'

'Yes.' Debbie was remembering Jim's last letter. It hadn't been exactly passionate, but then Jim never was, on paper. He wrote a lot about his work and had been at pains to tell her what hers would involve. She had also done a short course at a hospital for tropical diseases. It had all been extremely interesting and grist to her professional mill. The work side of her anticipated new life held no terrors for her.

'O.K., Elsa, thanks,' she said at length. 'I feel a lot better about everything now. I'm going to miss you, you know.'

'Well——' Elsa laughed—'find out if they want a radiographer out there. I'm all for a bit of a change. Of course these emergent countries are training their own staff now, aren't they?'

'Oh, yes. I think it's only in remote areas where hospitals are a bit understaffed. I'm supposed to coach two trainees as part of my job. Well, I'll have a shower and get dressed and then clear my things out of this room. I hope Pam will be happy here. I know I've been.'

'Pam and I will be as happy as two fighting cocks, when they're at each other's throats, that is. You know Pam and I are much too alike to get on. But it's only a temporary arrangement, thank God! After Pam I shall advertise for a complete stranger to share, I think. Preferably male and attractive.'

'Elsa!' Debbie was still chuckling as she stepped under the warm, refreshing shower.

Airports were awful places, Debbie pondered later that evening, as she signed the documents the hire-car man required to absolve her of any further responsibility for the Austin 1100 she had been using for the past three months. Elsa had bought her Triumph, and the cash had come in handy to buy a glamorous wardrobe of clothes suitable for the tropics and the rest had been transferred into letters of credit, etcetera. The hire-car man had to drive away quickly from the airport concourse, so Debbie gave him a couple of pounds and carried her two suitcases into the terminal herself. They weren't heavy, for most of her luggage had gone ahead and she expected it would be awaiting her at Okusha. An aircraft took off and she gritted her teeth at the row it made. All that noise and all that tonnage up in the air——! All that fuel——!

She forced her eyes open and proceeded to the departure clerk who was handling the Accra-Lagos flight, a girl who looked remarkably calm and cheerful. Well, of course, she wouldn't be travellling on the wretched thing, would she? Debbie was told the flight would be called at twenty-one-thirty for a twenty-two-fifteen departure, and was relieved of her luggage. It was still only nine o'clock and she wasn't going to dodge Vic Marchant deliberately, that would be too ridiculous and immature, but there was no sign of him and she wasn't exactly sorry. Maybe he had had too much to drink, too, last night, and couldn't remember everything that had happened between them.

She was holding a book Jim had sent her, entitled *Emergent Nigeria; its Peoples, Culture and Geography*. She had read it over and over recently, and some of the photogravure plates, taken by the author, were magnificent. She was looking at a picture of a group of Ibo women, wrapped in blue cotton skirts and with a matching turban round their heads. Every face was so black and every tooth, shown fully in ready grins, so white, that Debbie was quite entranced.

There were a great many West Indian nurses at St Matthew's, and also Indian and Pakistani staff, but she didn't think she had actually seen a true African.

She strolled into the bar and promptly saw quite a few of them, obviously waiting for the plane flight to be called, as was she. There were men and women, all very dark indeed, but only one was not in Western dress, and as the exception looked so very colourful, Debbie thought that was quite a pity.

She ordered the whisky Elsa had advised might give her some Dutch courage, and then saw Vic Marchant stroll in and look around. At first he didn't see her, but Debbie was aware of him in a most telling way. He was so good-looking, so aggressively masculine and so sure on both points that pure sensuality coursed for a moment through her veins and made her ashamed. It wasn't right to be going off to join one's fiancé and allowing another man to make one feel like that.

'Hello, Vic,' she said quickly and feigning surprise. 'What are you doing here? Meeting someone from somewhere?'

'I said I'd see you off, you silly old thing,' his latin-dark eyes proceeded to look her up and down. 'At one time I thought I wasn't going to be able to make it. I had a stupid woman went unaccountably into rigor.'

Debbie knew this was just his way of talking among professionals. He had been really concerned about that woman and her reaction, wouldn't have left her for anything unless she was safely out of trouble.

'I don't remember anything about you seeing me off,' Debbie lied. 'Did we arrange it last night? I was rather muzzy, I believe,' and she smiled sweetly. 'Anyway, it's very nice of you, Vic.'

'So you *are* still determined to go?' he asked, still with those eyes burning into hers. 'You may have been muzzy last night, as you call it, but they do say at such times people speak with absolute honesty. Last night you were not in love with Jim, had no desire to go out to Nigeria, but felt you must, if only to explain in person to Jim, and you led me to believe that you found me attractive. Well, Debbie, I'm here, and we're neither of us muzzy this time, so how do you feel about it now?'

She lowered her eyes, toyed with her whisky glass, looked up and saw all those coal-black faces behind Vic and then laughed, though somewhat shakily.

'Oh, Vic, I think we'd both better forget last night. Naturally I'm extremely nervous, I'm taking a big step, but whatever the future holds for me I'm sure we're not for each other in a thousand years. No, don't try to look hurt, Vic. It doesn't become you. I certainly find you attractive, but it takes more than that, doesn't it, to make a go of things? If I didn't go to Nigeria we'd probably have a torrid affair, which would simmer out like a volcanic eruption and then where would we be? You must have caught me in a weak moment last night. I need to be in Jim's arms—after all, I've lived like a nun for a year—and somehow I found myself in yours and I was extremely vulnerable. I'm not in love with you, Vic, and I'm equally certain you're not in love with me. You don't at this moment see me as the wife you would be coming home to, out of all women, do you? Ah, I see I've caught you there. Well, I'm not a here today and gone tomorrow sort of person emotionally, Vic. It's got to be for real with me. Jim's another very real person. If we're not for each other then we won't marry, even though I am at this moment wearing his ring on my finger.

'But I've got to go and see, and in any case there's my job to be done. You'll understand how important one's job can be, of all people. If we'd met at some other time I'm sure I would have enjoyed having an affair with you, because there's something inside me, like a trapped wild animal, which would have found expression in the excitement and sheer physicalness of it all.' Somehow Vic's hand had reached out and was clasping hers. 'But now it's all a bit late and I have to go. They're calling the flight.' She stood up uncertainly. 'Thanks for coming, anyway, Vic.'

'Am I allowed to kiss you goodbye?'

'I don't think that would be a good idea. Within a week I know you'll be leading some other girl up the garden path and I have no excuse for forgetting my loyalty to Jim on this occasion. My kisses must be for him. Excuse me, Vic, I have to go.'

She passed through into the departure lounge without a backward glance. So many more black faces now, even children's, so that the minority for once were white. There were a couple of nuns, a priest, middle-aged men who could be in business anywhere in the world and a fragile-looking white woman, old and desiccated, who looked as though she had never been out in the sun in her life, let alone having ties with Africa. The coloured people were mostly young, some looked like students, one or two of the families could be diplomats, in that they looked well heeled and spoke English with scarcely any trace of an accent. At the very last moment a tall, broad-shouldered young man came in still breathing heavily from running. He was European and bronzed and Debbie had an impression of piercingly blue eyes as he surveyed the throng. He was thickly and darkly thatched, and suddenly broke into a smile. Debbie thought he was smiling at her and decided to freeze, but he walked straight past her and wrung the hand of the priest. The two conversed in French, and as Debbie's French had only taken her to O level she couldn't make out much of what was said, and it was none of her business, anyway.

People were making last-minute purchases of English cigarettes, whisky and sherry and French perfume, but Debbie didn't know what to take Jim for a present. She said to a very dark-skinned man making a purchase, 'Excuse me, but what are you short of out there?'

He asked, very politely, 'Out where?'

A woman nearby laughed, and Debbie felt awful.

'I'm sorry,' she said miserably. 'I haven't been to Nigeria before and I wondered if it's difficult to buy liquor or—or toiletries. I have a friend working as a doctor in the bush, you see, and I'd like to take him something.'

'Oh, I see,' the coloured man relented slightly. 'Well, I'm Ghanaian myself, but I suppose one's needs out in the bush are much the same anywhere. I would take your friend a stock of after-shave and soap. Also a bottle of sherry would be nice. As a doctor he will be able to requisition brandy and such for his hospital.'

'Thank you. Thank you very much.'

'Not at all.'

Debbie made her purchases, aware of a blue-eyed scrutiny above her which drew her gaze despite herself.

'*Après vous, mademoiselle,*' he said with exaggerated patience, '*nous avons toute la nuit.*'

'*Pardonnez-moi,*' she said as haughtily as she could and made her selection of the after-shave more precipitately than she had intended. She wondered if Jim *was* a "Desert Oasis" sort of person or whether she would have done better to keep to a neutral sort of after-shave. As far as she remembered he had always seemed to smell of Wrights' Coal Tar. Even the soap was all highly perfumed and boxed, but she bought three boxes. She stalked away from under the Frenchman's nose, only to have him tap her on the shoulder a moment later to find him holding out her handbag.

'*Elle est necéssaire, n'est-ce pas?*'

'Thank you,' she said ungraciously, suddenly and unaccountably hating him with his laser beam eyes and wolfish grin. She objected to being laughed at, even in French. She was a trained physiotherapist, she wasn't

stupid and she wasn't clumsy, but because of her ner-
vousness she was being made to appear so.

When they marched out on to the tarmac, the great
bird which was to swallow them up seemed to rear up
menacingly, a heavier-than-air machine, which flew
simply because of a principle evolved by man, known
as aerodynamics. Why couldn't she be like most of the
other passengers who were mounting the gangway
almost gaily? The whisky didn't seem to have helped
at all and she had the usual desire to run away, so that
this time she actually turned round and bumped into
the Frenchman.

She said 'Pardonnez-moi,' again, and resolutely
climbed up an eternity of steps into the body of the
aircraft. When she was next aware of anything he was
on the seat next to her and was indicating that she
should fasten her seat-belt.

'Yes, I know,' she said somewhat sharply, and
fumbled with the locking catch.

Seven hours next to him, of all people, who looked
as if he didn't know what the word phobia meant.

She closed her eyes as the aircraft raced down the
runway, made a great deal of noise and became air-
borne. She ventured a peep and saw rows of lights far
below becoming more distant every moment.

'Well, at least we're up,' she murmured to herself,
and then began to feel sick. She tried deep breathing,
but it didn't work, and as soon as seat-belts could be
released had to make an undignified dash.

It was obviously going to seem a very long night.

Debbie decided the memories of that night's flight
would remain with her forever, sketched on her mind
indelibly and causing her perpetual agonies of embarrassment. It was not that she was the only one who, to
add to her fears of flying, had also been airsick. Two
of the coloured children had wailed constantly and one
of the stewardesses had been moving around quietly

handing out bags all over the aircraft and then removing them and their contents. It was just that Debbie,
refusing to ask for a bag, had made several dashes to
the rear of the plane, and had on one occasion fallen
into the Frenchman's lap, at the moment when he was
in conversation with the priest, as in the jumbo jet the
outside seats were in rows of threes, with fives and
fours down the middle, making the interior resemble
the body of a small cinema.

Debbie had booked her flight early enough to ensure
getting a window seat, but this proved no comfort
when it was too dark to see anything and there were
other people to scramble past in emergency.

The Frenchman had stood Debbie up and away from
him with iron-muscled arms and asked her in English
if she would care for a gangway seat. He explained to
the priest who in quick French was obviously most
agreeable, but Debbie, who was going to be sick at any
moment, mumbled that she didn't want to disturb
anyone and fled knowing that if she hadn't been feeling
so green she would have been as scarlet as a beetroot.

Another hour passed and then most seats were
tipped back, people had pillows and blankets and most
managed to sleep, but Debbie's eyes were burning
holes in her poor head. What a ghastly journey it was
turning out to be! She wasn't even frightened of crash-
ing any more. She had heard that seasick people craved
death, and in her own stomach's violence she even for-
got to listen for the drone of the jets, to note any change
in their rhythm. She had hung on and hung on and
then—oh, God!—it was threatening to happen again.

She looked around miserably. Most of the plane's
lights had been dimmed, only odd lights shone over the
seats of insomniacs, like herself. She saw her travelling
companion stretched out beside her, his head lolled in
her direction, and the steel-blue eyes were shut showing an incredible thickness of black lashes. She had no
time or inclination to admire him. The entire length of

his legs—he must have been at least six foot two—
occupied the gangway and she would have to climb
over him. She must go now!—*now*.

The plane gave one of those unaccountable lurches
as it met a turbulence of air and Debbie found herself
lying prone on the deck—as she afterwards heard it
called—lights clicked on all over the place, some in
annoyance, and then Debbie heard a stewardess's soft
voice.

'Are you all right, Miss Wyndham?'

'I—I tripped.' The Frenchman was glaring as he put
her back on her feet again. She had never seen such
eyes since she had ceased watching "Superman" as a
cartoon some years ago. 'I was on my way to the toilet,'
she told the stewardess, desperately.

'I'll go with you.'

Lights were snapped out again, irritably, and Debbie
allowed herself to lean against her companion.

They returned to the plane's galley and Debbie was
given a small tip-up seat.

'Now,' said the stewardess, whose name was Janet,
'let's see what we can do for you, eh? You ought to
know better than to keep retching on an empty stomach, especially with working in hospitals.'

'Yes, I realise. But you know how it is—one hates to
draw attention to oneself.'

At a quarter past six a sun like an orange rose out of
a black sky and suddenly it was light. There were no
preliminaries of grey dawn turning to pink and then
flame, as in more temperate zones, it was dark and
daylight within ten minutes, a harsh kind of daylight
which Debbie suspected was going to be very hot from
all she had read about it. Promptly at five past seven
the plane was circling Ikeja airport on the outskirts of
Lagos. Debbie could see the lagoons from which the
city got its name, and which were the breeding grounds
of the anopheline mosquito, which had accounted for
numerous British lives in its time, and against which

one dosed oneself with the deterrent drug proquanil for the duration of one's stay in such climes. Debbie knew that Jim had had a bad dose of malaria, and wondered if, busy as he no doubt was, he had become careless and not taken his proquanil. Anyway, she would soon be with him to remind him, in fact at any moment she should see Jim. At last something like emotion stirred within her, but it was also a kind of fear. She had felt it before, when anticipating visits to the dentist. It was something she had to go through knowing she would feel better at the end of it.

As it was full daylight she had no fears that the plane might miss the runway on this occasion, in fact she felt rather proud that she had lived safely through her phobia to make this landfall. Everybody poured down the gangway steps and walked into the reception halls of the airport. The heat was so blatant and intense and wet that Debbie poured sweat uninhibitedly and was going to ask Jim, as soon as she was reunited with her luggage and met him, if he would mind if she changed into something light and cool immediately. A drop of sweat even fell from her chin on to the passport the Nigerian immigration official was examining, and he smiled with a gash of ivory teeth to ask, 'Missie's first time in Nigeria? Ah, but you will soon get used to it, the blood becomes thin.'

Her blood felt like treacle at the moment and laboured through the chambers of her heart. She recalled that friends she had made at the Hospital for Tropical Diseases had advised her to travel out by boat the first time and so acclimatise herself gradually to heat. But at that time she had thought only of wanting to be with Jim as soon as possible. It is also impossible to imagine the soggy heat of West Africa or compare it with temperatures of places where the air is dry. It is the humidity which is a misery in itself.

One of her suitcases had its contents checked in detail by a Customs officer. He was young and seemed unnecessarily officious to Debbie, who was dying to get out of her soggy clothes and out into the fresh air.

She was one of the last to leave the Customs hall and at length emerged into an area like the forecourt of a station, where she was besieged by a number of ragged individuals who tugged at her suitcases. She said no, and tugged back. One of the young men said, 'You give dash, lady, I take case.' He succeeded in wrenching one of the cases from her and she rushed off after him, convinced she was going to collapse at any moment in that heat.

The headlong flight was stopped—yes, it was the Frenchman again—and he spoke sharply to the man with the suitcase, who sullenly set it down. Debbie looked around wildly for Jim, but though other passengers were going off surrounded by friends and relatives, Jim was nowhere to be seen and even the urchins and layabouts, who had been unable to sell their dubious services, were beginning to disperse and drift away.

'My friend doesn't seem to be here,' Debbie said miserably.

'No. Well, look here, it's your first time, isn't it?' She was amazed how good his English really was and nodded. 'There are so many reasons for hold-ups and delays here. I just have to see a friend off. I'll be back. Go in there and wait.' He nodded her towards the airport bar and behind him, in the burning sun, she could see the priest, now surrounded by a flock of nuns, being helped into a kind of charabanc. 'I won't be a minute.'

Debbie sat at a table and allowed her aching head to fall forward on to her wet arms. If the plane had been announced as leaving for London during the next few minutes she would have boarded it without a moment's hesitation or regret, that is if she could have summoned the strength, but as it was it took the Frenchman to lift up her head for her and survey her livid countenance for a long, hard moment. He then called a barman and touched her again to regard a glass of sizzling orange juice he had placed in front of her.

'Drink that, please,' he invited, and then produced two small tablets. 'Not drugs,' he smiled, 'only salt. I think that's what you need.'

She didn't argue but drank the liquid greedily and took the tablets. He ordered her another orange juice, but held his finger up warningly when she would have had a third.

'I think that should have replaced the liquid you have lost and the salt will help you retain it,' he explained, as to an idiot. 'We don't want you retaining too much fluid, do we?'

'I work in hospitals, you know,' she said at length, when she was feeling better. 'I'm a physiotherapist. I know one needs salt in this climate, but I naturally expected my friend to be waiting for me, and as he's a doctor he would no doubt have supplied me with all I needed. He should be along any minute. Don't let me keep you.'

'How interesting that your friend is a doctor!' said the Frenchman, apparently not aware that he was being snubbed. 'Is he in Lagos?'

'No. He's Surgical Officer at Okusha hospital,' Debbie said with some pride.

'Oh, no!' exclaimed the other. 'It can't be so!'

'But of course it's so!' Debbie said sharply. 'I should know where my fiancé is working! I'm going to work there too.' She pondered suddenly that this man seemed to have some knowledge of medicine. Last night he had wanted her to take something for her stomach and he had recently taken one look at her and produced the salt tablets without more ado. 'You're not a—a doctor at the hospital too, are you?' she asked.

'No, I am not a doctor,' he smiled. 'But I'm going to Okusha as well. A coincidence, no? Nigeria's a very big country. U.K. would fit into its pocket. I'm waiting for my assistant to bring my car. This is a country where one often has to—wait.'

He began to stuff an obviously well-used pipe.

'Do you mind?' he asked.

'No. Why should I mind?' She didn't know why she had to sound so ungracious. The man made her feel like a porcupine with raised spines.

'It helps to keep the flies away in this part of the world. Not that one ever quite succeeds. They quite outnumber us.'

At half past nine they were both still waiting and had introduced themselves, Deborah Wyndham and Jean-Marc Roland. Debbie had at last changed into the minimum of cotton underwear and a sleeveless dress, and felt a lot better, though outside the sun shone pitilessly so that a shimmer lay over the areas of the airport runways. She was pacing about and then observed, 'Isn't it hot? Is it always like this?'

'It's cooler if you remain still,' he told her. 'No, it's not particularly hot today. In April, if you are still here, you'll experience true heat. The humidity, which can be trying to newcomers, is with us always, whatever the temperature.'

Debbie sat down a little short-temperedly and looked at her watch.

'Wherever can Jim be?' she exclaimed.

'Probably still in Okusha,' said Jean-Marc Roland, biting on the stem of his pipe, which was now empty.

'Whatever do you mean?'

'Simply that this isn't U.K. and anything can happen or not. Mostly not. He probably hasn't received your letter, or whatever.'

'I not only sent him an airmail letter, telling him of the date and time of my arrival, but also a telegram, a couple of days ago.'

Jean-Marc Roland shrugged and chewed on his pipe.

'So what do you mean by that remark?'

'Airmail comes either to Lagos, or to Kano, in the north. Telegrams too. They are treated alike as ordinary mail and take their time to reach their destination. I shouldn't think you're being met today or, maybe, even tomorrow.'

Debbie felt an odd sinking in the pit of her stomach.

'You're trying to frighten me,' she accused, and then panic rose in her and took over. 'You don't like me and you're trying to frighten me. I think you're horrid.'

Jean-Marc Roland looked at her pityingly and with some impatience, rather as though she was a naughty and contrary child.

'Mademoiselle Wyndham, I have never in my life tried to frighten either a person or an animal. What do you think I am? I am giving you the facts as they are. Nigeria is still emerging, still exploring possibilities, still trying to develop its resources, with aid, of course. But Okusha is not the centre of Nigeria's universe and it therefore remains a rather neglected area in the national plan. It is a district where farmers and small-holders live and try to keep abreast of the survival rate with the help of people like your fiancé and myself. But we have no railhead in Okusha and mail and telegrams take time to reach us. Now I didn't create these conditions, I'm merely advising you of them. Okusha is a straggling, dusty village carved out of the middle of the bush by the British, who had an army camp there at one time. A tributary of the Niger flows through it, which floods during the rains and at all times ensures us a goodly supply of mosquitoes. You *must* know Okusha isn't London, or even—even Southend. Well——' he stood up, putting his pipe in his pocket—'there it is—and there, so I believe, is my car at last.'

A Land-Rover had drawn up and a very black man, dressed in a somewhat dandified way in a white silk shirt and drill slacks, got out and came to wring Jean-Marc Roland's hand. They both laughed a lot and slapped each other on the back.

'Please,' Debbie's voice interrupted, sounding very small and worried, 'I'm sorry, but what am I do to?'

'Oh, this is Simon Ungaro, from Okusha; Mademoiselle Wyndham.'

Simon now wrung her hand enthusiastically and looked waggish.

'Marc!' The dark eyes rolled in the black face, showing the whites. 'You never showed me your girl before. You planning to get married or something nice?'

Debbie flushed scarlet and Jean-Marc smiled a very thin, crooked smile.

'Nothing like that, Simon. Miss Wyndham has a fiancé at the hospital in Okusha. She rather expected to be met, but it doesn't seem like it. I've been telling her telegrams can take a week.'

'Oh, sure,' agreed Simon with a great laugh, 'if they arrive at all. I read in the *Daily Times* a week or so back how a mailman had burned his whole load for the Inegu district and spent his time under a banyan tree chewing tobacco instead of delivering the mail. He got to his village early and his wife was suspicious, then the medicine man said he was no good ju-ju because he was giving off bad odour. So then he gave himself up and was given six months' gaol. He'll smell better after that, I bet,' and Simon grinned again.

Debbie felt dizzy as she thought of things like medicine men and ju-ju in this day and age. She felt she had to be dreaming. She saw Simon and Jean-Marc again wringing each other's hands and then the Nigerian twinkled his fingers in her direction and dashed off into the sunlight. The Frenchman began to stow his gear in the Land-Rover, but he eventually came back and stood in front of her, huge and calm and somehow very cool, even in those temperatures.

'Well, Miss Wyndham, you asked me what you should do. Actually you have a few alternatives. You can stay here, in the hope that, despite my prognostications, your fiancé does arrive to pick you up. But if he doesn't, you cannot sleep here, and you would quickly become a wreck without proper toilet facilities and a bed. Alternatively I could run you to a hotel, where you can stay until he does arrive. You could leave word at the information desk of your whereabouts. Your final alternative is that you could still leave word at the information desk and accompany me to Okusha. I'm leaving now. I expect to arrive in the early hours of the morning if I can make good time. Should you decide to go to a hotel to stay, I will notify your fiancé of your arrival and then it will be up to him to fetch you. Now you must make up your mind, and fairly quickly.'

'I—I'll go with you,' Debbie decided, rather wretchedly, and without more ado Jean-Marc went to collect her two suitcases and put them in the back of the Land-Rover.

'Right, hop in!' he invited, holding the door of the passenger side of the cab open.

'But aren't we waiting for Simon?' she asked him. 'Isn't he coming with us?'

'Simon has taken an airport bus into Lagos to enjoy some leave, having held the fort while I took mine, Miss Wyndham. Why? Does it make any difference? Don't you want to be alone with me?'

She looked at him, as though expecting to be able to see some flaw in his character. His dark hair was almost blue in its blackness and those sharp blue eyes of his held her gaze with a flicker of impertinent laughter as they met. He wore a bush-shirt over matching fawn slacks and boots into which the legs of his slacks were tucked, probably anti-snake boots, she decided, fearing the worst of her new environment.

'Good gracious,' she exclaimed, climing up into the cab, 'I'm not afraid of *you*, Mr Roland!'

'Splendid!' he said, also climbing into the cab, and donning dark glasses from one of his capacious pockets. 'I assure you that you hold no interest for me other than as a somewhat reluctant passenger, mademoiselle. I will deliver you to your fiancé, who no doubt sees all manner of charms in you.'

The air was crackling with hostility as he turned on the ignition, let in the clutch, found gear and roared away.

'Oh, how I do hate *him*!' Debbie was thinking silently so that she scarcely noticed that it was Africa which was flashing past on either side of them.

CHAPTER TWO

JEAN-MARC ROLAND proceeded to bring Debbie's education on Nigeria up to date. 'The majority of these forty-odd million are Muslims, and there is little education for girls. A creature who is a chattel, and has no soul with which to enhance heaven, need not concern men overmuch while she is on earth, apart from fulfilling her natural functions and making her lords and masters happy.'

'You really enjoyed telling me that,' Debbie accused, 'as though you more than half believed it yourself.'

His smile of masculine superiority enraged her.

'Anyway, what are you, a Frenchman, doing here? Nigeria was a British colony and you have lots of ex-colonies where you could well occupy yourself, I have no doubt.'

Jean-Marc's strong eyebrows became twin arches of amused inquiry.

'Oh? What makes you think I am a Frenchman, then?'

'Well, aren't you? The way you speak French, like a native, and your conversation with that French priest. I—naturally I assumed you were French,' and she tossed her head.

'Then you were wrong and wrong again in your conclusions, and I don't think you're a young lady who likes very much to be wrong. My country has no ex-colonies nor desires any. I am Swiss, and I come from Neuchâtel, therefore I speak French.'

'Well, it's the same thing really, isn't it? You're practically French.'

'No, I am not. There are German-speaking Swiss who are *not* Germans, and never will be; Italian-speaking Swiss and French-speaking Swiss and a few who speak ancient Romanisch, but we are united by the fact that we are all Swiss and very definitely independent, both as a country and a people. I'm happy to be able to add to the education of at least one female.'

Debbie saw a Nigerian knocked off his bike by another cyclist. There was a great deal of noise and excitement but no real damage.

'I'm sorry,' was eventually torn from her. 'Obviously the Swiss are a proud people. I mean, they have a right to be proud—the International Red Cross and all that.'

'Yes. We do not make wars, but we do not shrink from entering the firing lines of those who do with our comforts and our aid. We do not manufacture atom bombs but pharmaceuticals.'

'And watches,' Debbie added.

'*And* watches,' he smiled his sardonic smile again. 'Forgive me for forgetting that we are best known to the world for our watches.'

'Now you're trying to make me feel small.' Somehow Debbie could not leave bad enough alone. She had to make it worse. 'Of course I know Switzerland manufactures pharmaceuticals. I work in hospitals. Ciba-

Geigy—Sandoz and so on. I *do* know that. But other people manufacture pharmaceuticals, too, whereas Swiss watches are the best in the world.'

'And some of the worst,' said Jean-Marc. 'Pop watches are manufactured which are no better than plastic toys. I've seen a lot of those here, in the villages, and felt ashamed. By the way,' he added loftily, 'if it is of any interest to you my mother was English. She died last year, expectedly. Even Swiss pharmaceuticals couldn't save her.'

'I'm sorry.' Debbie lowered her eyes.

'No, don't be sorry. I'm not. She suffered for a long time. Also the priest I conversed with wasn't French, either. He was Belgian, a casualty from the Congo, now Zaïre. He looks after the Catholic community in our area, though his headquarters are in Cameroon. Do you find the sunlight trying?'

She was screwing up her eyes again.

'The glare off the road and from windscreens and things is very sharp,' she said. 'I suppose I'll get used to it.'

He handed her his sunglasses and waved them at her when she would have refused.

'Go on, wear them or you'll get a headache. I *am* used to it.'

'Well, thanks.' She put on the glasses which promptly fell into her lap, tried again and this time caught them in her hands.

'You've got a bigger head than I have,' she decided. 'They don't fit.'

'What you really mean is that I've got a big head, period. Use some initiative, woman! There are some tissues in front of you. Make plugs of them to put between your ears and the ear-pieces. There, isn't that better? Anyway, there isn't much more of this road and then there'll be little glare to bother you. I propose to stop in Igena for lunch, and then make as good time as possible. Have a good lunch, because we won't be stopping for dinner and I'll be driving all night.'

'All night?' Debbie echoed. In her surprise she dislodged the precariously fixed sunglasses, which were expensive Polaroid ones, and they fell with an ominous crack to the floor of the vehicle. When she picked up the frames one lens was splintered into fragments and the remaining one cracked.

'Oh, dear!' she said miserably. 'I wouldn't blame you, frankly, if you were wishing me a thousand miles away at this moment. I've been nothing but an unmitigated nuisance to you since we met.'

'Despite any wishes I might have,' Jean-Marc Roland said quietly, 'you *are* here and we'd better make the best of it. Not to cry over spilt milk is a good English proverb, and it is equally useless to bewail broken glasses. Collect any pieces you can find and wrap them in a tissue. We don't want to cut your feet, and I see you are not wearing stockings.'

'Should I be, in this heat?' Debbie asked.

'Not if you don't mind nice big red bite marks showing. When we reach the bush you won't even see the things that bite you.'

'Perhaps I should have asked your advice, Mr Roland,' Debbie decided, 'and instead of giving you an opportunity of frightening me again, have simply asked if—in your opinion—I should put stockings on when we stop for lunch in Igena?'

'If I were you, yes, I would. I would also wear a blouse with long sleeves, much as that dress becomes you.'

Surprised by this into an unexpected blush, Debbie said that yes, she had such a blouse, and would put it on.

The great road went on into infinity, but shortly after this conversation the Land-Rover turned off to the right and there was now two-way traffic to watch out for, and much of it driven erratically. Jean-Marc was constantly snatching at the wheel to avoid an overloaded 'Mammy-wagon' or a juggernaut racing to join the motorway that would lead it to Apapa wharf to discharge its load of groundnuts, palm-oil or tin or rubber.

Occasionally the road ran through a village, or maybe such villages had grown up because of the road, as they appeared ramshackle and rather slummy places with peeling mud and adobe houses and, often, completely naked children. The only solid-looking buildings would be the bank and maybe an official's house or offices.

'There seems to be a high incidence of umbilical hernia here,' Debbie commented. 'Surely that can be prevented nowadays?'

'Give them time,' Jean-Marc advised. 'There is modern medicine, yes, but there are also a lot of old beliefs and customs. I don't think it's yet usual for the average peasant woman to have her baby in a hospital, or even to be under the care of a district nurse during her pregnancy. When she goes into labour, it's much simpler to send for the old woman who has always assisted at deliveries than to try to get qualified help. Such help may be hundreds of miles distant, anyway. This is a big country. So the old woman, who may have at least been persuaded to wash her hands first, but, being unable to read, knowing little more than her predecessors throughout tribal history, will bring the child into the world and cut the umbilical cord with either a piece of glass or a knife, if somebody has given her one, and in one case out of every three the child will develop a hernia.

'We won't think how many women die of septicaemia, a few will, and others will survive to be treated by some roving medical team in the area. There just aren't enough trained personnel to guarantee a nationally backed health service. If you can get to a hospital you'll be treated for your ailment and advised as to future behaviour, but if you can't you'll either die or get better. It's as simple as that.'

'I'm beginning to understand a bit how Jim must be feeling,' Debbie said as though to herself, her eyes looking inwards. 'Just lately his letters have been—well, full of shop-talk and he seems to be professionally frustrated. He's hardly written of anything but the patients and the diseases and what I'll be expected to do. I——'

'You mean they haven't been love-letters?' Jean-Marc asked with a wry smile. 'I can understand that. A doctor in a bush hospital has one heck of a job on his hands and he no doubt feels drowned in problems half the time. If he has come from a spanking London hospital it would take him a year to get over the shock. But when you're actually on hand—well, it'll be different, won't it? You can share his problems and work alongside him. I wonder if I've met your fiancé? I have dined a couple of times at the hospital.'

'His name's Brant. Jim Brant.'

Jean-Marc narrowly avoided running over a lean cur of a dog, which darted for cover with a yelp of alarm.

'Oh, poor thing!' Debbie exclaimed. 'She has three puppies in the ditch there. She's probably foraging for them.'

'And she's probably rabid,' said her companion. 'I'll ring the veterinary officer for this area when we reach Igena and he can get them seen to.'

'You mean injected?' Debbie asked. 'Immunised?'

Jean-Marc gave her a wry glance. 'And then find the puppies good homes?' he asked. 'No chance. They'll be destroyed.'

Debbie said nothing. She realised she was in a strange land with, no doubt, strange but necessary customs. She remembered reading something on her immigration form about the import of domestic animals, how all dogs had to have a valid certificate of immunisation against rabies and other diseases. She thought of Britain with its comfortable, sleek, coddled

canine population, and of the R.S.P.C.A. who were
there to see nobody mistreated any animal, and how
stray dogs were kept fed and housed in kennels, by
voluntary organisations, until alternative homes could
be found for them. It all seemed suddenly far away
and here there was still the feel of nature in the raw, as
though even the bush on either side of the twisting
road could reach out and take over whenever it felt like
it.

'So have you met Jim?' she asked. 'Before we saw
the dog you were saying . . . He has thick, sort of tawny
hair and brownish eyes with flecks of green in them.'

'I don't go out to dinner with the intention of gazing
deeply into men's eyes.' Jean-Marc said. 'I met a pink-
ish sort of peeling chap, but I don't really remember
him. Dr Oduloru I like a lot, and there is a good-looking young woman with black hair at the hospital. I
have looked into *her* eyes and they said keep off. I
didn't notice their colour.'

'You mean a European?'

'There *are* a few of us around. Being masochistic by
nature we're the ones who answer all those adverts for
jobs in horrible places. I mean, your fiancé would never
have got a job in the hospital in Lagos. All the bright
local boys who've trained in London will certainly see
to that. *You* might have got a job in Lagos. I don't
think physiotherapists are so thick on the ground.'

'I find you extremely cynical, Mr Roland,' said
Debbie, still thinking about the black-haired European
woman working in Jim's hospital whom he had failed
to mention in their correspondence.

'I prefer to be called a realist, Miss Wyndham. This
is an African country run by Africans for Africans. We
are merely incidental to their development and pros-
perity, and would do well to remember that.'

Hovels began to appear on each side of the road and
the bush had been cleared to provide small areas of
cultivation or pasture for a few cows or goats.

'That's how much trouble emanates,' said Jean-Marc, 'where the landowners are still fierely independent in their very small way. Soon we come to a large co-operative where things are organised a bit better for the common good. Many boys are going into agricultural colleges, which is a good thing, as this country is extremely fertile and can be made to produce all its own needs and have some to export to less fortunate African countries. Here's the co-operative now.'

Debbie saw fields rich with maize, growing in orderly rows, and others filled with the fading heads of large sunflowers. A group of young women were collecting the seed heads from the flowers and laughed and waved at the Land-Rover.

'Girls are a valuable labour force,' explained Jean-Marc. 'Their brothers are, no doubt, getting a higher education, but where young men from poorer families *are* working in the co-operatives, they work in their own groups. Boys and girls over a certain age are strictly segregated. Girls are still an asset to their families and are not allowed to form relationships with the opposite sex of their own accord. Nowadays they wouldn't admit it, but there is still a bride price to be paid. Some of the men are in their middle thirties before they can afford to get married. Of course, in the cities, things are more relaxed. The universities accept both sexes. But I doubt any friendship formed in university will end in marriage without the full consent of both families. There are still tribal influences at work here. Chiefs are extremely highly thought of. Not all the old ways were bad ones, as we Europeans should remember when we discard things because we label them decadent.'

Soon there were pastures with cattle in them. They were cattle with humps but quite plump and shiny. Jean-Marc was driving slowly now, obviously interested in the scenery.

'Are you,' asked Debbie, 'by any chance a vet, Mr Roland?'

He shot a quick glance at her.

'I didn't think you were interested,' he said, 'but yes, you could call me that. Okusha area Senior Veterinary Officer, in full,' and he smiled. 'There is a bit more to my job than giving puppies their shots of Epivax and removing a fishbone from pussie's throat.'

'I suppose there is,' said Debbie levelly, 'the way you were looking at those cattle as—as I've seen my father look at racehorses. His ambition was always to breed them, but he lost a lot of money before he got to that stage and we all had to settle for less in the end. I was reading for my B.Sc. in medical school, but I realised I couldn't afford to stay the course, so I became what I am. My sister, who was reading pure mathematics at Oxford, came down and got a job in a bank. Mother went back into nursing—she was a hospital Sister when she married; she still is, though she only works days and she's not resident. My father had allowed the practice to run down a bit; he was a country G.P., and always rode to hounds from which I suppose he got his love of horses.

'We had this big steeplechaser in a barn at the back of our house, eating his head off when Father wasn't riding him, and having a famous cousin who had been placed in the Grand National twice. Father offered Chestnut's services to those who were interested, but of all the foals he sired none made the headlines, and meanwhile a spry young doctor had settled in the area and Father was losing patients by the dozen. When the barn caught fire and Chestnut was literally roasted, I don't think Father ever recovered from the shock. He was ten years older than Mother but by no means an old man—sixty-four, I think—but he suddenly looked old and within a year he died. I know they put the cause of death as hypertension on the certificate, but I always think he loved that blessed horse so much, and nursed his dreams of running a stud farm so dearly, that he just died of the disappointment of it all, especially as he felt he'd failed us.'

Debbie suddenly stopped speaking, aware that for the first time in her life she was telling a perfect stranger the intimacies usually reserved for family friends and close acquaintances.

'I'm sorry, too,' said Jean-Marc, 'that you have lost such a fine character as your father must have been.' She felt herself warming towards him. 'I can see him, doing the job he had to do to live, but distracted by this passion of his for horses, and one in particular, of which he expected such great things, and which had no doubt inherited only some of the qualities which made his cousin famous, and it *is* a kind of fame to be placed twice in the most exacting steeplechase in the world. No doubt your father did suffer from hypertension—he sounds a bucolic type—and when you get hypertension together with shock and disappointment and financial worries, you can die quite easily. I think you've all responded admirably; your mother must be quite a woman and you girls have shown you can rise to the occasion. I suppose you were intending to become a doctor?'

'Yes. I——'

'Well, don't knock the job you're doing. It's a good job.'

'I don't. I enjoy it and it can be very rewarding.'

'I'm sorry, too, about—Chestnut, was his name?'

'We girls called him that. He was a lovely chestnut colour but a vicious brute. Only Father could handle him. His real name in the stud book was Ashenden Viscount.'

'Do you ride?'

'Yes, but only school hacks. I never rode Chestnut. It's years since I rode, anyway.'

'You should have mastered Chestnut. Never allow a domestic animal to dominate you.'

'You didn't know that brute!'

'I would have made it my business to get to know him, and on my terms.'

'I'm sure you would.' Bighead, she was thinking, again not liking him much. 'Ah, a bit of decent road again! I was just getting used to being bumped around.'

'The road carries us into Igena, where we'll have some lunch, and then continues about twelve miles beyond as far as we're concerned. Unfortunately we have to leave it and return to our bumping, after that. I'm sorry, I can't help the road. I'm a vet, not a civil engineer.'

'Oh, I'm not blaming you. In a way I suppose I'm enjoying myself. I've got a headache from that awful night and the glare, but I keep marvelling at things I see, things I suppose some people would give their ears to see. Some trees way back there, covered in purple blossoms—I suppose they were jacarandas? Well, it isn't every day you see a jacaranda, is it?'

The savannah, when they reached it, seemed to go on and on. The vastness of the terrain to somebody from an island, like Britain, was difficult to accept. Debbie kept imagining just over the horizon they must eventually see the sea.

They had stopped under what Jean-Marc described as an acacia tree for a much-needed drink, which turned out to be hot tea from a thermos flask packed by the hotel staff where they had taken lunch. The hot drink made one sweat, but Debbie knew that sweating is nature's own cooling system and must be encouraged. With her second cup he gave her another salt tablet.

'That should see you through now,' he said. 'When your blood has thinned down you won't need such things. Ready?'

'Oh, must we?' Debbie was stretched out in the long yellow grass and looking up at a sky which simply couldn't be as blue as it was. It was a technicolour sky, exaggerated by the white lace fragments of thin clouds here and there.

'Yes, we really must,' said Jean-Marc, and then Debbie gave a sudden squeal and literally leapt up. Big red ants, at least an inch in length, were crawling all over her legs and nipping her strongly. One had reached the tenderness of her thigh and she slapped it down and jumped and wriggled until she was free of the invasion.

'Why didn't you warn me?' she asked a grinning Jean-Marc. 'Now that I think of it *you* didn't sit down. You leaned against the car and drank your tea.'

'Warn you about ants in Africa?' he asked her. 'On your own admission you've read a book or two. In case you didn't know, it's their country, too, and they come in all shapes and sizes, night and day. The red ants and the soldier ants are most aggressive, and if you look around you can see ant-hills everywhere. There are ants which one rarely sees but which can under-mine the foundations of a house and cause it to col-lapse. There are marauders which come out at night and have very sweet tooths, if one can say such a thing in the plural, and will literally drown themselves in your breakfast marmalade if you're unwary enough to leave it around. I'm sorry you got nipped, but I honestly didn't think. I've been out here five years and have forgotten there are still people who imagine waysides are picnic places. Not here, so be warned. If I forget to warn you later, by night we'll be beset by mosquitoes, so be prepared. Now let's get on.'

The road went on and on and still on, sometimes in a state of terrible disrepair with huge potholes to cicumnavigate, or bump through if the banks were high on either side, and sometimes actually boasting a sur-face if they were approaching a town. Once in a very lonely place a solitary man in a ragged singlet, shorts and with a red sweat-rag round his dusky brow was filling up one of the potholes with stones, but stood back to grin and shout out as the Land-Rover went by.

'*Alafia!*'

'*Alafia!*' responded Jean-Marc.

'*Elinko!*'

'*Elinko!*'

'*Omonko!*'

'*Omonko!*'

'*Owa*!' from the distance.

'*Owa*!' Jean-Marc called back.

'What was all that?' asked Debbie, who suspected she had been asleep.

'He's a Yoruba man and I know a bit of the Yoruba dialect. Simon, my assistant, is a Yoruba. That was the equivalent of hello, how's your father, how's your mother, how are the wife and kids and goodbye.'

'How *are* the wife and kids?' Debbie asked. The shadows were getting very long now, and the landscape was green, well wooded, almost forested and very hot.

'The questions are merely polite and hypothetical.' Jean-Marc said. 'One doesn't answer them literally. The English say how do you do, and one doesn't reply 'Very badly', or 'Quite well', one says how do you do in return. But if you really want to know, my wife and thirteen kids are thriving.'

Debbie pondered and decided she had been snubbed.

'Gracious!' she said. 'I wasn't intending to be nosey, merely sociable. You know I have a fiancé and I told you all about my family. I don't know why, really, because you're obviously doing me some sort of favour and don't want to be sociable at all.'

'I *am* rather tired,' Jean-Marc said in reply, 'and I don't think I'm feeling very sociable at the moment, if you don't mind. You'll have to forgive me. We're running an hour later than I had planned and I must keep my wits about me. In half an hour it will be dark. Do go to sleep if you can.'

'I don't suppose it's any use my offering to drive for

a bit? No, I thought not. I wouldn't know the way, would I? All right, I'll shut up even if I don't sleep.'

'Thanks for the offer, all the same,' he said a moment later. 'If you did know the way, I would take advantage of it. I have nothing against women drivers.'

Debbie forbore to say something scathing like, 'Well, that's a comfort!' and settled her head against the canvas side of the mica window on her side. She saw water, brown and turgid, dashing itself against the supports of a bridge, and then heard the sudden hollowness of the sound as the tyres sped over the bridge. Darkness dropped literally like a cloak. One moment an orange shone through the trees and then the car's headlights were on and those same trees took on menacing shapes and put out roots apparently to trip one.

It was possible to believe in demons lurking in that rain forest. In the headlights some trees appeared to have heads, with twig hairs sprouting from them, and others had reaching arms and fingers which snatched at the Land-Rover as it passed. Once a pair of red, unwinking animal eyes stared at Debbie's own from the darkness.

'Are there lions hereabouts?' she asked nervously.

'Unfortunately no, from an ecological point of view. There are some in zoos and national parks, of course, but lions are not bush animals. They like the savannah with an occasional tree for shade. There are plenty in East Africa still.'

'I just saw an animal staring at us. Great red eyes.'

He smiled in the darkness. 'It could have been an odd leopard. They still do exist here, but mostly have strolled over the border.' He was thinking to himself that it was most likely to have been a stray dog hunting for its supper. Even pet dogs had eyes which glowed red at night, but he felt his companion was in need of a thrill after the boredom of the long journey and so he wouldn't disappoint her.

She grew drowsy soon afterwards and didn't quite

know where she was or what she was doing when she was hurled like a limp rag doll the extent her seat-belt would allow, and back again. She automatically felt her bruised ribs and remembered where she was as she heard Jean-Marc cursing energetically below his breath. Now recollecting fully what she was about, she asked, 'Anything wrong, Mr Roland? What's up?'

'Sorry about that. Waking you up, I mean. Are you O.K.?'

'Yes, I'm O.K., I think. And you?'

'A bit winded, nothing worse. We've blown a tyre. It's a damned nuisance. I'll have to change the wheel. Are you anything of a mechanic?'

'No. I always sent my car to the nearest garage.'

'Yes, I might have known. I'll bet you know how every joint in the human body functions but not how to use a spanner.'

'Well, we don't use spanners on human joints, exactly. I'll do all I can to help. Is that fair enough?'

'Yes. Sorry to be such a bear, but I could have done without this. We'd better get to work. The blow-out's on your side, at the front. Your job will be to hold the torch while I do the work.'

'I think I can manage that,' she said relievedly.

Once the torch, a huge, heavy square thing, like a carriage lamp, was switched on, he dowsed the head-lights to conserve the battery and collected his tools together, a jack, a polythene bag and the spare wheel, which he kicked and criticised.

'There's not enough air in that for my liking. Just wait till I get hold of Mr Simon Ungaro! I've told him always to keep our transport in tip-top condition, in-cluding pressure in spare tyres. Could you stand just there, please, and keep the torch steady?'

Debbie stood as he asked, though the torch was heavy and she held it in both hands, and watched as her companion jacked up the Land-Rover and began to loosen the bolts on the damaged wheel. All seemed to be going so well that her attention wandered. The smell invading her nostrils must surely be the smell of Africa? It was thick and pungent and sweet and rancid at one and the same time. She had read many books and knew that the fertility of the heart of this continent fed on the continual decay, so that trees would topple and rot and provide the food for other saplings and growths. It was a natural revolution, as a wheel revolves, it was a cycle which had worked nature's way since the beginning of time. Only man interfered with the cycle and cleared away the bush—or forest—whatever one cared to call it, to plant his crops, and because he left open spaces once he had garnered in his millet, or maize, the sun dried, the rains and winds came and the once rich earth was eroded away, which was what came of interfering with nature. Of course nowadays people were more aware of their environment and what it meant to life and living; people were planning more on long-term bases now, rather than thinking only of tomorrow, or next week, and——

'Miss Wyndham!' came sharply into her ears, so that she jumped.

'Yes, Mr Roland?'

'Do you think you could hold the torch still? There's a nut here which is one hell of a lulu to shift and I must be able to see what I'm doing.'

'I'm sorry. Is that better? You know your English is remarkably idiomatic? Fancy a Swiss knowing what a lulu is!'

He gave what she imagined was a faint snort.

'I did occasionally talk with my mother,' he said acidly, no doubt because he was tired and fed-up and trying to do a job in un-ideal circumstances. She did her best to make allowances for him and held the torch steady, even when he hurt his thumb and let fly with a few rather strong words, English and as idiomatic as 'lulu' had been.

She fancied that if she had asked 'Did that hurt?'

he might have said even worse things. She felt it better to bite her tongue and simply hold the torch.

Behind her was a deep ditch in which water gurgled, and beyond that the thickness of the bush. Suddenly, she didn't know why, she remembered those red eyes gazing so unwinkingly at the passing car and now couldn't get them out of her mind. Why, at this moment a leopard might be behind her, watching as unwinkingly, silently crouching to spring.

'Could you——?' Jean-Marc waved towards her and she jumped unwittingly. 'What's *up*?' he asked in exasperation. 'I've nearly got this damned thing, so hold still! A bit to your right.'

So jittery had Debbie become, however, that she took a step backwards and lost her balance on the edge of the ditch. The torch made the first splash and she made the second, a big one. The torch shone for a moment under water, then went out. There was now only darkness and silence save for Debbie's whimperings of sheer human misery. Strong arms hauled her to her feet, hands felt her over and made sure her bones were intact, then she was shoved against the spare tyre leaning against the Land-Rover and the second rescue operation went on for the torch.

There were sounds of furious clicking, but nothing happened, and if hostility can be said to have a smell then it was all round them, thick as a London fog.

'I'm sorry,' said Debbie thinly.

'So am I.'

'I—I don't know what to say.'

'In that case I wouldn't say a thing.'

'We can't go on, can we? I've spoilt things.'

'We can't go on, period. I can't drive on three wheels and a prayer.'

'I wish I could *do* something.'

'You can. Shut up and climb in the back and go to sleep. You'll find a net and a blanket.'

'But——'

'For once just *do as you're asked*!'

Debbie somehow felt her way round to the tailboard of the Land-Rover and heaved herself over. She hurt her knee on something sharp and cried out, then she felt a blanket and below it what must be a mosquito net, and rolled herself in both, still crying quietly to herself, for she was soaked to the skin and, though she couldn't really believe it, was actually feeling cold.

She heard Jean-Marc clumping up and down outside for some time and then he climbed into the cab of the vehicle and there was silence apart from noises from the bush. Something howled far off; a leopard? jackal? she wasn't sure of the fauna of the area. She thought she heard an owl and the rustle of bat-wings. She gave a self-pitying sniff.

After about an hour she heard Jean-Marc take another walk, and, as she was too uncomfortable to sleep, she simply allowed her thoughts to wander. She was going through the contents of her handbag when she saw his face, with considerable five o'clock shadow making his jaw quite blue, looking over the tailboard at her. She was holding a cigarette-lighter, which was a gift from long ago, though she didn't smoke. It was made from two of the old halfpennies and a brass nut and had been given by a grateful patient who was clever at making such novelties.

'You'd better put that thing out if you've finished with it,' said Jean-Marc. 'Lighter fuel is scarce out here.'

She obeyed in silence.

'I'm sorry if I upset you,' he continued, though now she couldn't see him and wondered if the words were hurting him to speak. 'It wasn't really your fault. Anybody can have an accident.'

'Oh, yes,' she said quietly, 'it *was* my fault. I allowed my imagination to wander and became jittery. I got it into my stupid head that a leopard was about to have me for supper and didn't know my right from my left, my back from my front. It was my fault all right.'

In the darkness he smiled ruefully.

'Leopards aren't that thick on the ground here-abouts,' he told her. 'I hope I didn't lead you to think otherwise. But let's not talk about the might-have-been and accept the facts. We're stuck here till daylight——'

'Well, Mr Roland, finding the lighter made me think of something else. In one of my cases I have a torch. Just a small bedside torch, but if would help——?'

'No, I don't think I could actually change that wheel by the light of a small torch, though thanks very much for the offer, Miss Wyndham. It shows you're now trying to be helpful and I appreciate that. Daylight is about three hours off and I think it would be a good idea for us both to get some sleep, don't you? Also it might be better for you to arrive in the daylight than in the middle of the night, especially if you're not actually expected. There'll only be a watchman and the night nurse on duty at the hospital, and you could have proved a bit of an embarrassment, I suppose, if they didn't know what to do with you. Also you must be wet, and that's not very nice. It can be cool at night when the harmattan blows. You don't actually hear the wind blowing, but it feels like a cold vapour by the time it reaches here from the Sahara. Are you cold?'

Deborah allowed herself the luxury of a shiver.

'A bit,' she said.

'Do you mind if I come in?'

'Er—no.' She felt him vault over the tailboard and then he struck a match, and, as it died, stuck two khaki garments at her.

'Strip and put those on. They'll be big, but at least they're dry and comfortable.'

She managed to wriggle out of her wet things and dry herself with parts that weren't as wet as others. She pulled on a pair of shorts and a bush shirt which came to her knees.

'There, that's better!' Being dry felt suddenly heavenly.

'Right! Now we've got to share the blanket and the net. I've only got one of each.'

A faint doubt in her mind was crushed as he placed what appeared to be a haversack between them and promptly fell asleep. It was some time before she followed suit, but finally she relaxed and was in dreamland.

Hours later Debbie stepped out of the Land-Rover and looked at the hospital where she was to work for at least the next six months. It had three wings, joined together, and the fourth side of what was a square was composed of a high mud and adobe wall, whitewashed, with a gateway in the middle through which Jean-Marc had driven. There were verandas facing on to the compound, where there were flowerbeds of red and yellow hibiscus and blue agapanthus lilies. On one of the verandas a Nigerian nurse was helping a patient into a reclining chair, and other patients were already looking with interest at the visitors.

'So that's that,' said Jean-Marc, dumping her bags. 'I'll be off.'

Only when she saw the Land-Rover disappearing out of the gateway did she come to her senses and run after it calling, 'Stop! How do I thank you? How *can* I thank you?'

Her questions were left hanging in the air and she went back into the compound, picked up a case in each hand and climbed a flight of steps, for the hospital was on stilts and there was daylight between it and the earth.

Before her was a door marked ENTRANCE, but it stood open, so Deborah edged inside. She overcame a sudden feeling of unutterable shyness to knock on a door marked OFFICE and from behind which she heard voices. An English voice called 'Come in!' and she turned the handle. She couldn't have felt more nervous if she had been a member of the Light Brigade entering the dreaded valley of death.

The first person Debbie saw was Jim, complete with white coat as she remembered him. Funny how she remembered him better as a doctor, after a year, than as her fiancé. The thick, leonine hair she remembered appeared a little bleached and the hazel eyes, light brown, shot with green flecks, gazed at her first in incredulity and then lit up in something like relief. Her first instinct was to run into his arms, to actually recollect him by the feel of him, but she recalled just in time that Jim was never affectionate in public, or even in front of a witness. And there was a witness in the room, of whose lavender fragrance and pristine white uniform Debbie was aware to her right, though she hadn't yet taken her eyes off Jim's face, wondering how he *was* going to greet her after all this time.

In the event he reached out and took both her hands in his.

'Well, Debbie, welcome to Okusha! It's such a load off my mind that you're actually here. You see, we just received your telegram this morning and realised you were actually in Nigeria, and heaven knew what you'd be doing or thinking because you'd be expecting to be met. We were worried sick, weren't we, Sister? Debbie, you know Sister Eve Meadows?'

Debbie at last turned and held out her hand to Sister Meadows, who had also once been at Matthew's. Debbie hadn't known her awfully well, hadn't come across her a great deal. Had she been a night superintendent or something? She *had* seen her, of course, and Sister Meadows was quite a striking-looking person. Her hair was raven black, smoothly parted and braided behind, and her eyes were a surprising light grey, almost pale.

Debbie said as they shook hands, 'Well, what a small world! I mean, fancy you being here in Okusha too, Sister!'

'It was Eve who first told me about the place,' Jim interposed, 'and got me interested. We love it here, don't we, Eve? I hope you're going to like it too, Debbie. You can do a lot of good.'

Debbie looked hungrily at him again. She wanted to be alone with him, to really say hello in love's own way. Surely he was feeling the same way?

'Incidentally, how did you get here?' he asked, apparently genuinely interested.

'I came with your veterinary officer, Mr Roland, who was on the same flight. He said you wouldn't have got my telegram, and he was right.'

She was about to elaborate when Sister Meadows asked suddenly, 'Where did you spend the night, Miss Wyndham?'

She didn't call me Debbie, the other thought. She and I are going to be formal with each other.

'Most of it in the Land-Rover, actually. We broke down. Otherwise we had intended driving all night.'

'I'm sure *he* would contrive to break down,' said Sister Meadows, with a kind of sweet reasonableness which was vaguely offensive. 'Trust him!'

'Oh, but we did actually break down,' Debbie insisted. 'A tyre blew out. I know a busted tyre when I see one. I had to hold a torch while he changed the wheel, only I dropped it in a ditch and then fell in myself.' As Sister still smiled she added, 'And if anybody thinks it was *that* sort of a night then they should know that Jean-Marc Roland and I were at loggerheads from the very start. We kept each other in a state of constant irritation and I never feared for my virtue for one instant.'

Jim said, soothingly, 'Don't fly off the handle, my dear. Sister has heard the chap has a bit of a reputation, that's all. She's only concerned for your welfare. But as you are here, safe and sound——'

'And very hungry and thirsty,' Debbie added. 'Jim,

can't you come and have some breakfast with me somewhere?' She tugged his hand rather as a child tugs at a favourite uncle.

'Well, actually we've had breakfast. We eat early and we eat late here.' He seemed at last to sense that some kind of storm was boiling up inside his fiancée and that he had better pacify her. 'But I'll take you to your quarters and ask one of the stewards to bring you something. That's if Sister can carry on without me for fifteen minutes. O.K., Eve?'

'Certainly, Doctor. You trot along. The main thing is that Miss Wyndham's here and you don't have to make that tiresome journey to the coast. I'll see if Dr Oduloru's ready for rounds and explain the position.'

A black steward boy in a pyjama-like suit had already picked up Debbie's bags and followed the couple as they went the length of a corridor and then out of a small door at the rear. Behind the hospital was another compound and bungalow-like dwellings at intervals on its perimeter.

'The hospital used to be a barracks,' Jim explained, 'when the British were here, and the bungalows were officers' quarters. We have had to dig out the tennis court and restore it, because we have to make our own entertainment here, and a bit of honest exercise is as good as anything. We also play table-tennis and billiards. However, I'll show you to your quarters. Your house is a bit pokey, but quite new. Anyway, you won't be spending much time in it, only to sleep.' He stopped outside a small hut still smelling of whitewash. The grass around it had been scythed, but there was no garden as such.

'A physiotherapist is a bit of a novelty at Okusha,' Jim said, almost apologetically, 'and I suppose you'll just have to prove yourself, Debbie. I have quite a nice bungalow, and so has Eve, who has some standing as Sister in Charge, but——'

'The physiotherapist can be shoved into a hut, eh?'

Debbie asked wryly, and stepped inside her quarters. 'Very functional,' she commented, noting the teak table with its four legs in jars of paraffin—no doubt to deter ants and termites; its two upright bentwood chairs and single easy chair with shabby, faded cushions, and the cubicle beyond, which contained a single bed, with a mosquito net tucked away above, a bedside table and a single chair. She was glad to see her large tin trunk in the middle of the floor. 'Where do I keep my clothes?' she asked, looking round.

'Well——' Jim looked stumped for a moment. 'There isn't much room, is there? I should—if I were you, Debbie, I'd use that trunk as a wardrobe. You have to think about all sorts of pests here, moths and—and mould. Mould's the biggest nuisance. Your shoes can turn green overnight. I think your trunk should be mothproof and you can hang things out to air, or rather, your boy can when we get one for you. Until then you'll share a hospital steward. Your arrival has really taken us all by surprise. Your house was thrown up in a week, after I got you last letter.'

'Surprise, Jim?' she asked, turning to confront him, then noticed the steward still standing holding her cases. 'Can't we do without him?'

'Thank you, Henry,' Jim said dismissively. 'Missie will unpack her own things. Bring breakfast for Missie. Tea or coffee?' he asked Debbie.

'Coffee would be heaven. I'm thirsty.'

'Big jug coffee, Henry. Quick sharp.'

'Very good, Doctor.'

At long last Debbie threw herself at Jim and felt his arms slowly embrace her. She lifted her face and pouted her lips. Jim kissed her and drew back.

'Oh, Jim, for God's sake! After a whole year can't you do better than that?'

He did do better, but still her lips pressed after his had ceased. It seemed to her that she was seeking some core of experience of which this was only the outer skin. But maybe Jim had forgotten her a little, too, and was still shy.

'All this nonsense,' she took refuge in saying, 'of my arrival being a surprise! You knew six months ago I was planning to follow you and I gave you the estimated date of my arrival which I said I would confirm by telegram. As I've heard telegrams are inclined to arrive with the ordinary mail here, you could be pretty sure that yesterday morning I'd be at Lagos Airport, so why the surprise?'

'It's such a big step,' said Jim, 'that you could easily have changed your mind at the last minute. I couldn't believe you were coming until you were actually standing there. But I'm glad to see you, Debbie, I really am.'

She wanted to kiss him again, at that, but was afraid of sensing him trying to play up to her expectations of him. Let him make the advances, she decided.

'How long has Sister Meadows been out here?' she asked.

'Two months longer than me. It was when she was talking about her proposed appointment that I got the bug, too.'

'I didn't even know about Sister Meadows being out here. You never mentioned her. I rather fancied you and I would be the only Europeans for miles and that would rather—er—draw us together or—or the other thing.'

'What do you mean by "the other thing", Debbie?'

'Well, if we saw enough of each other, the only two Europeans in the hospital, we'd either rush into marriage—though I know you once said you would never do that—or grow to hate the sight of each other. To me, my coming out here was significant to our relationship.'

'And isn't it?' he asked her.

'Well, we can hardly sneak off together in the evenings and leave Sister all on her own, can we? At

Matthew's we could spend quite a bit of time together, and nobody was upset, but I suspect I'm going to see less of you here, Jim.'

'But that's ridiculous, Debbie. We're going to see heaps of each other every day. I know what you're hinting, that our personal relationship might be affected, but I thought I made it quite clear to you that we wouldn't decide about our marriage until you'd had this experience with me. After all, if it's going to be my life, and you hate it, we may have to think about things very seriously.'

'Do you mean we might have to break our engagement or that you would come back to England?'

'I mean we'd have to talk, Debbie, like sane and sensible people. Oh, come on, darling!' It was the first time since her arrival that he had used that endearment and she looked up sharply. 'Here you are just arrived, not even unpacked, and already you want me to decide the future. I'm not a rusher, Debbie. I never have been. You're not going to panic me into changing now.'

She leaned against him suddenly and put her arms around him. She could hear the steady rhythm of his heart and her right hand stole up and found the moist damp of his hairline against his ear.

'Oh, no, you don't!' He was laughing but his hands were like steel as he put her away from him. 'You're not going to get me into a state when I'm supposed to be on duty. Dr Oduloru's a good man to work for, but he expects us all to pull our weight. He'll understand my taking fifteen minutes off to show you your house but not to indulge in a love-scene. He'd think there was a time and place for all that.'

'Oh, there is,' Debbie said quite gaily. 'We turn on the tap at ten-thirty and off at eleven, because we must get a good night's sleep, what? Up early to do our jolly old duty and no footling old nonsense. Somerset Maugham got it all wrong, didn't he? His characters in the tropics were simply sex fiends.'

Fortunately at that moment the boy Henry re-appeared with a tray, from which he removed a cloth, for Jim's face was a picture.

'Well, get your breakfast and enjoy it,' he said. 'If you're interested, all the staff meet in the Director's room for a drink and a sandwich at a quarter to one, before siesta, but we'll understand if you don't come this once. I'll know you're catching up on your sleep. But we're all back in the hospital by four, if you care to come over and look round. Eve understands that you're dining with me tonight at my house. O.K.? As we're a mixture of African, Asian and European we always eat our evening meal in our quarters. You'll get used to the food. I'll leave you to it, then, Debbie.'

'Yes.' She smiled up at him as Henry obligingly poured her first cup of coffee and slid a grapefruit, a plate of toast and a tightly screwed-down jar of mar-malade on to the table. 'Off you go, Jim. I expect I am rather tired. I'll see you some time.'

She was almost glad to see him go, and eagerly dismissed Henry, too, with the observation that he must have other duties.

'Yes, missie, me very important hospital steward. Me see all kitchen kept clean. Missie get own boy, maybe from Okusha town, some time soon.'

Henry pattered off on sandalled feet and Debbie gulped her coffee and poked at a segment of grapefruit. Then she allowed herself to relax and become aware of the vacuum within, not of hunger but of disappoint-ment and disillusionment. After a year there should have been something electrifying and climactic be-tween her and Jim—she did, after all, wear his ring on her finger—but instead he had pushed her another six months away by refusing to play her game of lovers' meeting.

'Oh, no,' he had said, 'you don't get me into a state when I'm supposed to be on duty!' After twelve months of living like a nun, until that last night before

her departure, she had come out here expecting some
kind of delayed fusion which had simply not happened.
Jim's first glance on her had been that of relief from a
great anxiety the telegram had placed on him, and she
had even had to contrive their being alone together for
ten minutes, which he would apparently cheerfully
have forgone because he was supposed to be on duty.
She knew, without being told, that Jim and Eve
Meadows normally dined together, eating the same
European-type food, and that Sister was being very
kind in allowing the sweethearts a couple of hours in
which to become re-acquainted on this evening. But
she also suspected that by tomorrow night it would be
considered quite normal for them to dine as a threesome, and that when Jim was on duty he would be a
rigid disciplinarian of his own passions, as he always
had been.

As she had nestled up to him that first time she had
felt tremors of excitement surging through him, but if
they were so controllable then she wondered if Jim
was really capable of such raging desire as would carry
all before it like a river in spate. She had never been a
promiscuous person—she had heard the chatter of girls
to whom the whole concept of human love was a date,
a cuddle, a cheap thrill and all over until the next time—
but she nursed a deep conviction that she was an all-
or-nothing person. She had to love and be loved to
depths that remained unplumbed and heights to which
there were no bounds. The past year had made her
forget Jim in many ways, as he had probably forgotten
her, but if the fact was that there was not sufficient
about him for her to know, then it was just as well he
had laid down the condition that they work together
for six months before there was any committal. Perhaps
Jim really was wise, and she was the impetuous one.
Only time, she decided, would tell.

At last, having settled her mind a little, or at least
accepted the facts of the moment, she took interest in

the food in front of her and the rest of the coffee. She remembered what Jean-Marc Roland had said about the 'sweet-toothed ants' and screwed the top of the marmalade jar on tightly. She wondered if he had rolled into bed or shaved and was now about his day's work. It was a pity she hadn't thanked him properly, but it was only what he would have expected of her, anyway, and so he would not be disappointed.

She wondered if Jim had it in him to make her feel so nervous and apprehensive of him in his anger as Jean-Marc Roland had done. As he had hauled her out of the ditch last night, felt her over and then discovered the ruined torch she had almost expected him to strike her; had obeyed him like a whimpering cur dog when he had told her to get into the car and go to sleep. She had never been bossed like that before, or could the word be 'mastered'? Then there had been something about her relief, when he had appeared to apologise and forgive her, that had been akin to a dog licking its master's hand.

'Oh, but I really hated that man,' she now told herself. 'He was detestable, actually. I wonder how Sister Meadows knows about his supposed reputation and what it is? Well, I don't really. I'm not at all interested. I suppose I'd better do a bit of unpacking and have a look round. What do I do about bathing, for instance?'

She found a sort of lean-to shed at the side of the house with a zinc bath in it and over it was a kind of grid. As there was a handle to pull, she stripped and pulled, a shower of water came down over her in one electrifying surge and then no more. All the pulling she could muster produced no more water, so she soaped herself, dried off and dressed in fresh clothes, including cool cotton uniform tights, and decided that there was a steward boy who possibly carried water to the shower-rooms once a day and with this she would have to make do.

Her little hut—she couldn't think of it as a house—

certainly seemed to be an afterthought as it was isolated from the other bungalows, outside the hedge surrounding the tennis court. This hedge was a frangipani, covered in little pink flowers and very fragrant, with variegated leaves. A barbed wire fence gave her what she imagined would be ten feet of garden on three sides eventually, and the fourth side was the frangipani hedge of the tennis court. She wondered if the fence was to keep her in or other visitors out, and looked towards the bush behind her. It was very dense, but a clearly delineated path led into it. She was sure Jim wouldn't let her live where wild animals could get at her, that the bush was probably innocent of predators.

Just outside the small gate in the wire she discovered a stand-pipe carrying water and a well-worn area of earth round it which probably meant that the path out of the bush brought villagers seeking water. As she pondered she heard shrill little voices and two children appeared; one, a girl, with a blue wrap gracefully draped across her flat chest and carrying a brass pot on her blue-turbanned head. She dragged a naked male child, about three years old, by the hand. Both stopped as they saw Debbie, and the whites of their eyes looked startlingly brilliant in their black faces.

The little boy tore himself free and fled. The little girl looked nervous, one hand had automatically reached up to steady the heavy brass pot, but she held her ground and stared.

'Come on!' Debbie encouraged. 'Get your water.' She waved in the direction of the pipe.

The girl didn't move. She looked like a small carved ebony statuette, graceful and old beyond her ten or so years.

Debbie realised that as she was standing by the standpipe she might be thought to be laying claim to it, and went back through her gate, again invited the girl to approach and went towards her hut. When she turned again the girl was at the tap and this time they exchanged smiles. The girl somehow heaved up the brass pot, which must have been heavy by now, and put it back on her head. She contrived to turn and wave and disappeared into the darkness of the bush, slim to the point of thinness, but obviously as tough as steel wire.

'Oh, it might not be so bad here,' Debbie told herself. 'If the people are like that and——' a blue and yellow bird swooped into the sunlight, caught a fly and was lost to view again. A tulip tree was covered in creamy blossoms—'there are other compensations.'

A great weariness overcame her, and it was so very hot with the day now well advanced. She went to her cubicle-like bedroom and lay down on the top of the bedclothes. She only meant to think, but was soon in a deep, satisfying sleep.

CHAPTER THREE

DEBBIE presented herself at the hospital in one of her clean white cotton overalls, with its distinctive green epaulettes and belt, feeling not a little nervous, and was greeted by a coffee-coloured young doctor with the distinguished good looks of his race. His eyes were dark and thickly lashed, his hair gleamed as though it had been oiled and his lips were well-curved, almost sensual.

He held out the warm hand of welcome.

'You must be Miss Wyndham? How is dear old Blighty, then? Dr Ranji Saba at your service.' He let go of her hand and put his own together in the *namaste* of the Hindu.

'England's pretty miserable, I should think, at this time of year,' Debbie answered him, amused by that reference to 'Blighty'. 'Did you train in the U.K., Doctor?'

'Oh, no, not me. I am Nigerian born, believe it or not. My father has a shoe shop chain in Lagos. I have not even been to old Blighty. But my grandfather, who emigrated here, never stopped talking about it. He was bearer to a British officer, you see, in his own youth, in Delhi. That is why, you will see, I am so fair-skinned. We of Delhi are not a dark-skinned people. Not that I am saying, you understand, that darker people are not as good. Oh, dear, I will get myself into such a knot in just one moment. No, I returned to Delhi to do my training, and though my father wanted me to go to Blighty to work in London for a year or so—it is very important to have worked in London or Edinburgh, you know—I was young and impetuous, still, and I wanted to come home, which is here, though I must be confusing you. An Indian who thinks of Nigeria as home. Also there was a girl——'

'Oh, so you're married, Doctor?'

'No, alas! That one was not right for me. My horoscope said marriage was not for me at present, so here I am, but not to worry. I am gaining so much experience professionally.'

'Have you a speciality, Dr Saba?'

'Well, not really, though I wrote my thesis for my M.D. (an M.D. Delhi, mind, not London) in deficiency diseases, of which there are plenty in India, and, as one comes further into the bush, here. So I am a pretty useful fellow to have around, and now I will introduce you to our Director. This is his office and I believe he is in.'

Dr Saba knocked on a door and a deep basso-profundo of a voice invited the knocker to 'Come!'

'I think you will be wishing to know our new member of staff, sir? Miss Wyndham, a physiotherapist from England. London, England.'

Dr Oduloru could have been Paul Robeson, or Paul Robeson playing a doctor. He was large, very black, ugly and bespectacled, but there was a kindness about the eyes, immediately, and he rose and set a chair for Debbie where he could see her properly.

'Well, Miss Wyndham, I'm glad you have arrived. I won't ask you how you like our country, because most Europeans hate it at first and then, surprisingly, it seems to grow on them. People who swear they'll never return, after a two-year spell of employment, almost invariably come back for more. So we must have something, mustn't we? Of course your first tour is, unfortunately, very short, only six months. That may not give you sufficient time to settle down. You'll feel the heat, and then you'll hate the rains and whoomph! you'll be gone. But your appointment was really a bit of an experiment. We have been so busy in other ways making up for lost time that we have not got around to training sufficient people like you to do the after-care in our hospitals. We are short of radiologists, path. lab. technicians and dispensers, so that we are inclined to be jacks-of-all-trades. But you will be mainly at my disposal as I'm the orthopaedic specialist.'

Debbie's brows rose and she glanced at the papers on the desk.

'Oh!' he laughed his deep brown laugh. 'You think a hospital director sits on his behind and directs, eh? Not in Okusha. We all do a full-time job of work and get the paper-work done somehow. Also we are all called "Doctor". None of your "Mister" for surgeons. Come!' he called a little sharply as there was another knock at the door.

Jim stood, looking flustered, 'I'm sorry, sir. I thought I'd given Miss Wyndham to understand that I would show her round the hospital. You must be busy.'

'Not too busy to welcome our new staff member,' said Dr Oduloru. 'It is an extremely pretty face to see.' He and Debbie exchanged smiles and then she rose, knowing better than to impose herself and Jim on his hospitality.

'What did you go and see him for?' Jim asked quite sharply, in the corridor. 'He always has an hour in his office at this time, an hour which is sacrosanct.'

'Well, actually, Dr Saba introduced me, and the Director was *most charming*,' Debbie said with emphasis.

'What else could he do? Tell you to get to hell out of it? And that loony Saba should have known better. Anyway, what did you talk about?'

'I don't really remember. It was just a very pleasant exchange, I think.'

'Did you tell him about us?'

'What about us?'

'That we were engaged?'

Debbie thought for a moment before answering. 'Doesn't he know, then?'

'No, he doesn't. Nobody does except Eve. When we were discussing your appointment out here I wanted you to get it on merit and not because it must be presumed I wanted you with me for personal reasons. He knows that we worked in the same hospital, of course.'

'And did you, really?' Debbie asked, still thoughtfully.

'Did I what?' Jim asked a little sharply.

'Did you, in your heart of hearts, want me with you for personal reasons?'

'What a daft question to ask! Really, Debbie, you seem determined to try to provoke me at every opportunity! The answer is that of course I did. I am just the same, it's you who have changed.'

Debbie looked at him with the ripe chestnuts which were her eyes. With her pale gold hair, their colour always came as a bit of a surprise, and she saw him swallow involuntarily.

'Well, now I'll answer your question, Jim. No, I didn't tell Dr Oduloru about us, or Dr Saba. So if that's the way you think it should be I'll certainly cooperate. Before we continue with our tour, perhaps you'd better have this.'

She took off her engagement ring with its twists of gold ending in twin diamond serpent eyes and held it out to him. Her finger felt surprisingly cold and naked without it.

'Here, what's this?' he asked, with a questioning smile. 'Have we had a row, or something serious? Oh, heavens, I can't explain things to you here in a hospital corridor. Later . . . Now, come this way. This is the men's ward.' He hurried her along, and Debbie was aware of a sudden hush and black woolly heads on pristine pillows turning to behold her. Blue-frocked black nurses with white aprons were busy about the place. A male steward was cleaning windows and another ran a mop over the plain wooden floor. 'All hospital servants are male,' Jim said. 'In Africa it's mainly the boys who are trained to do housework—for other people, that is. They would never dream of doing a hand's turn at home. It's just in recent years that girls have been employed as nannies, and, as you see, they take to nursing. But not many girls here have O levels, let alone four of them, so we have to pick the brightest girls we can find and make the most of them. Better practical nurses you'll never find, but they couldn't pass an exam for toffee. I must hand it to Eve, she does wonders with these girls. Within a few weeks she has them giving injections and taking temps and B.P.s How she does it I'll never know! Hello, Maussa! How's it feeling today? Better? Good! Kwiki? Sore, eh? It will be for a day or two.

'These are my surgical patients at this end,' he explained to Debbie, 'and Oduloru's too, of course. We only have two wards, one male and one female, so we keep the medicals at one end and the surgicals at the other. We have a couple of side-wards where we put the very ill, usually the dying, and we have a small isolation ward of four beds built off the other wing.

Shall we go and see the women? Sister's probably over there.'

Debbie tried not to think that he strode out across the hot compound the more jauntily on account of that fact. They were hailed from the patients well enough to sit out on the verandas and then a boy in a clean white pyjama suit came running up.

'Doctor, sah! This the lady I assist?'

'Oh, hello, Oliver. Debbie, may I introduce Oliver Dwaro, who hopes to assist you in your work and learn from you—Miss Wyndham.'

'How do you do, Oliver,' and Debbie held out her hand.

'I'm fine, miss, real fine. Glad to know you.'

'Oliver has been working at the hospital for about five years as a steward and is ambitious. If he shows any application towards physiotherapy then the Director may send him to Lagos for further training. You will have a female assistant too, from the local convent, Tundi Abele. Educationally she's quite sound but needs a vocation. So see what you can do with both of them, eh?'

'I like Oliver,' said Debbie, as the boy went back to attending to the needs of the patients on the verandas.

Sister was on the women's ward talking to her staff nurse. She immediately came to meet the visitors with a sweet smile of welcome which, Debbie decided, though feeling she was biased, did not reach those strange, pale eyes of hers. Her dress was of silver-grey cotton, square-necked and short-sleeved, though her cap was old, an extravagantly frilled Matthew's Sister's cap, with strings which tied demurely under her chin.

'We had a thrill one day about a couple of months ago,' said Jim, 'didn't we, Sister? A film unit was doing some work in the area and the producer went down with malaria. He was brought here and the rest of the crew decided to do an extra feature on the hospital. They were rather impressed to see us both and a hos-

pital apparently functioning in the middle of nowhere
so efficiently. So for just one day we became film-stars,
didn't we, Eve?'

'I presume Drs Oduloru and Saba were in it, too?'
Debbie asked sweetly. She was wondering if Jim
thought the same as she did as Sister had come down
the ward in her immaculate uniform and demure yet
ostentatious cap, that she looked simply too good to be
true. A film-star ward Sister, in fact. And yet the hospital *was* functioning and she was the senior nursing
administrator here. The patients all looked clean and
comfortable and even happy where they were well
enough. Only one bed was screened and a soft moaning
came from within.

'We're having our first baby,' Sister said cheerfully,
'and we're only sixteen, and we still have a long way to
go, I'm afraid.' It was only now Debbie realised Sister
was talking about the patient behind the screens. 'I'm
glad we got her, otherwise old women would have
given her something to help the birth along and
probably caused a prolapse and Lord knows what else.
Well, we're going to let nature take its course and do a
bit more shouting yet. But we'll have a fine baby at the
end of it and no infected umbilicus.'

'That's the spirit,' Jim applauded.

Debbie fancied that Sister Meadows could see the
end product quite clearly, a healthy little baby all
neatly tied off and wrapped in hospital clothes, but
that she couldn't so clearly see a frightened girl of sixteen, cut off from her kinfolk, and as alarmed by the
contractions of labour as anybody else for the first
time.

'Perhaps I could help the girl with her breathing,
sort of keep her company?' Debbie suggested.

'Well——' Jim's eyes approved her but deferred to
Sister.

'I think not, Miss Wyndham,' that lady said very
quietly. 'You're not on official duty yet, and it would

be very spoiling for the other patients to see a perfectly natural confinement getting individual treatment. Our mother-to-be can safely be left to get on with it at present. When the time comes she shall have our undivided attention. Don't worry on that score. By the way, Doctor, wouldn't you like to carry on with your work? I'll take Miss Wyndham round the ward.'

'Right-ho. See you this evening, Debbie, if not before. We dine at nine, but come for an aperitif first.'

'Now, Miss Wyndham,' Sister said in her business-like voice, 'you'd probably like to see some of the patients and be told what's wrong with them so you'll know if your services will be useful to them or not. Drs Saba and Iloro, the two physicians, if you can call them that with their limited experience and qualifications,' she smiled apologetically as she said this as though more in sorrow than anger, 'won't have known the luxury of working with a physiotherapist before. You'll have to show them what you can do with medical cases. Yes, Doctor?' her voice had suddenly sharpened and Debbie saw that she was addressing herself to a dark, woolly-haired young man in a white doctor's coat.

'I wondered, Sister, if it is convenient for me to set up that saline drip now? I can fit it in——'

'It certainly is not, Doctor. Come back in half an hour and I'll have everything ready for you. As you see, I'm busy with Miss Wyndham.'

Debbie stuck out her hand impulsively and said, 'Dr Iloro? I'm Deborah Wyndham, the new physiotherapist.'

'How do you do. So nice to see you, Miss Wyndham.' He glanced nervously back at Sister. 'Very well, Sister, in half an hour.'

'I could have shoved off,' Debbie said when he had gone. 'After all, the work of the ward comes first.'

'The work of the ward *is* going on,' Sister said, glancing around approvingly, where the staff nurse was now dragging her dressing trolley with her and two other young girls were making beds. 'I would never allow it to stop for anything. But I won't have Dr Iloro imagining I am at his beck and call just when he feels like doing something. He has had very little hospital experience and must learn that we have ways of doing things.'

'As a Nigerian might he not resent——?'

'Oh, *he's* not a Nigerian,' Sister said dismissively. 'He's a Ugandan and had barely taken his finals when he fled for political reasons. We don't even know that he passed his finals, and personally I very much doubt it. That's why I always insist on being present when he cuts down to a vein or gives an injection.'

'Doesn't that make him nervous?' Debbie asked.

'I don't know, and I don't very much care. My patients must come first. These are Dr Oduloru's patients. Now this is a rather sad case.' An old woman lay with eyes shut, apparently unaware of their presence. She had thin sticks of limbs and her black skin was a greyish colour dotted with white, like freckles in reverse. Sister picked up one of the arms to allow Debbie to examine the rash. 'That means she's had many bouts of malaria in her time. Of course malaria doesn't kill them, they accept it as a fact of life as we accept 'flu. When she was brought in here she was unable to walk, and said somebody had put a bad ju-ju on her and that she would die. Her family asked who would want to put a ju-ju on an old granny who had always been highly respected, but they do believe in such things on the sly, you know. Especially the old. Anyway, she's been lying there day after day, not eating, and Dr Oduloru can't find anything wrong with her, but she's accepting death. She's now so dehydrated that I've decided to fight the ju-ju a bit longer, hence Dr Iloro's saline drip. But she'll die in the end, you'll see, of ignorance and superstition, nothing else.'

They went from bed to bed. Complaints Debbie had

only heard about during her course at the hospital for tropical diseases became facts under her nose. A bad case of bilharzia filiariasis, a bush child with sleeping sickness, a young woman recovering from snake-bite.

'Well, Miss Wyndham,' Sister said at last with finality, 'I must get one of my nurses to help me prepare for Dr Iloro's visit. A half an hour I said and half an hour it shall be. I hope you've found it interesting, but I must get on now.'

'Yes, thank you,' said Debbie, at a bit of a loss. 'Thank you very much, Sister.'

'Oh,' the other smiled suddenly, deprecatingly, 'I know you'll have been told to wander around as you please, but I wouldn't, if I were you. I'd keep right out of the way and take advantage of your few days' leave. If you appear on the wards a member of the staff will feel in duty bound to escort you, and as you can imagine, we're all very busy.'

'I understand, Sister,' Debbie said.

She went back to her little house without even trying to see Jim again. She felt hot and sticky, but there was no water in her shower. She was also very thirsty, desperate for a cup of tea and managed to run down a steward who turned out to be working in the Director's bungalow. He smiled kindly upon her, however.

'Look, what's your name?' she asked? 'I'm Deborah Wyndham, the new physiotherapist. I live over there.'

'Yes, I know that, missie. My master very glad you come. Director very busy doctor. My name Joshua.'

'I know Dr Oduloru is very busy and I hope I can help him. Just now I wonder if you could help me, Joshua? I have no water in my shower and I would like a cup of tea. I don't know what to do about these things as I don't seem to have anybody looking after me.'

'Ah, let us go and see, missie. The Director has it in his mind that you are needing a boy. Never fear, when he is not so busy he will see to it.'

They arrived at the house where Joshua disappeared up into the roof and then proceeded to carry up buckets of water from the stand-pipe.

'There, missie, is your next shower. Now, where is your kitchen?' They prowled about outside and next to the shower-room was a small, empty place which Debbie had thought of as a store-room. One side of it stood open. 'Nothing in kitchen at all,' Joshua announced. 'That is very bad. Missie give me few minutes. I will be back.'

'I don't want to take you from your own work, Joshua.'

'Don't worry, missie. No chop for tonight. I not doing a thing just now.'

In ten minutes Joshua reappeared with an open basket on his woolly head and a can in one hand.

'Missie!' he greeted, swinging down the basket with natural expertise. 'Come now! We fix up kitchen.'

From the basket he took a flat, paraffin-burning affair with two cooking rings, which he placed on a stone block in a corner of the outbuilding. Next he produced a couple of old pans, one without a handle, a chipped cup and saucer and screwed-up papers containing tea and sugar. He also produced a tin of condensed milk.

'Now we soon boil water and make tea,' he said, and proceeded to pour kerosene into the small cooker. Debbie, meanwhile, had taken one of the pans to fill with water. Joshua appeared to snatch it from her with a telling frown. 'Missie no do steward boy's work,' he said quite sharply. 'Missie work hospital, make leg better, *not* carry water. Director be most angry to know this t'ing.'

'Sorry,' said Debbie. 'I don't want to make anybody angry.'

Back in the kitchen Joshua busily scooped tea into a battered old enamel tea-pot which had also appeared out of the basket and poured on the boiling water triumphantly.

'Tray. Where tray?' he asked, looking round.

'I don't think I've got one,' said Debbie.

'Missie go sit in room. I come quick with tea. Find tray.'

Debbie did as she was told and eventually Joshua arrived with the lid of a biscuit tin for a tray. He had punctured the tin of milk and triumphantly commenced to pour.

'Delicious!' said Debbie, and really meant it. 'Thank you so much, Joshua. Where do I have to take all these things back to?'

'Oh, missie can have. All finished with. Hospital Director has butane-cooker now. Is good tea?'

'Very good tea. I hope I get as good a boy as you, Joshua.'

'Oh!' and the lad promptly covered his eyes with his hands and laughed. 'I go now, missie. You got shower. You got tea. O.K.?'

'O.K. And thank you, very much.'

Debbie was at the stand-pipe, washing out her cup and saucer and rinsing out the tea-pot, hoping Joshua would not catch her doing such things for herself, when she jumped at the sound of a voice.

'*Alafia!*'

She beheld the girl in blue she had met earlier in the day, again with a brass pot on her head, and smiled.

'*Alafia!*' she replied.

'*Elinko!*' went on the girl.

Debbie hesitated, remembering how Jean-Marc Roland had rattled off a whole sequence of such greetings, and smiled again, standing aside.

'I speak some English talk,' the child said, 'I go to school.'

'Oh, good!' Debbie applauded. 'What's your name?'

'Dina.'

'That's a very nice name,' Debbie smiled.

'Your name?' the child pointed. 'What your name?'

'Deborah.'

'De-bor-ah!' Dina seemed to find this excruciatingly funny and laughed. 'What you do?' she demanded, and snatched the cup and saucer from the other, examining them sharply. 'Not clean,' she decided, and sought about her. The soil was sandy hereabouts and she proceeded to use the sandy soil as one would use scouring powder back home. When she had rinsed the crockery under the tap it gleamed. She then took the tea-pot, grimaced over the stain the tannin in the tea-pot had caused and gave that the same treatment. Now the inside of the teapot was a shining white and the outside blue, save where the enamel was chipped and showed black. She collected the items together, but didn't hand them over. Instead she asked, 'You live here?' and as Debbie nodded, opened the gate in the wire and went through. She couldn't have been more than ten, but looked about her in an adult way and occasionally frowned. She straightened the covers on the bed.

'You got bad steward-boy,' she finally concluded. 'He not doing work properly.'

'I haven't got one at all, not yet,' said Debbie, wondering if she should have opened her house to a stranger, even such a friendly little stranger as this one seemed to be.

'Not got steward-boy?' asked Dina, aghast. 'De-bor-ah, are you lady doctor? Nurse?'

'No, I'm not either. I help the doctors.'

'Very bad you not got steward-boy.'

'I know, but I'll get one soon. Dina, I think you should go now.'

'I go. I go in just a tick.' Debbie wondered where the child had picked up such an idiomatic saying and followed her into the bedroom where her new friend was reaching up and pulling down the mosquito net, tucking it under the mattress. 'Soon skeeter come,' she said solemnly. 'Too late if he already under net. Steward-boy should to these things. Very bad you no have steward-boy. Go now. Goodbye, De-bor-ah!'

They shook hands solemnly, and the child left, closing the gate carefully after her and reaching over to shoot the bolt. Debbie heard the tap running into the brass pot and then the clearing was empty and silent and the sun fast dipping into the trees.

Remembering how suddenly darkness fell in these parts Debbie looked how the house was lit. There were no light switches, but she found an old-fashioned paraffin lamp in a corner. The container was dry, however, so she quickly dashed round to her 'kitchen' hoping Joshua had left the can of paraffin—or kerosene as it was called here. He had, and she silently blessed him as she filled the lamp and then looked round desperately for matches. None, and now the shadows were lengthening alarmingly. She remembered the lighter in her bag and lit the lamp. Now all seemed much more reassuring. Before she should forget she looked for—and found—the bedside torch she had brought with her. She put it on the chair by her bed alongside a novel she had brought to read. Now, with light, she felt much more organised and went off with the lamp to take her evening shower. Though all day she had been aware of a slight breeze through all the intensity of the sun's heat, now, with darkness, it had dropped and it was as though a shroud had also dropped with the night. The damp was tangible; the walls of the shower-room sparkled with condensation and outside the trees dripped. All was still and silent and very wet.

Even after her shower Debbie sweated more than she had done all day. She dressed carefully for Jim's eyes. Perhaps this evening it would feel so different when they were actually alone in his bungalow. She had been told about the climate and even her evening dresses were of cotton, with patterns of beautiful broderie anglaise here and there. This evening she wore a green dress, and though the only mirror she could find hung on a wall and bore legends of a drug firm on its frame, she had to approve what she saw. She hoped Jim would. It was still too early to go and seek him out. He wouldn't leave the hospital until eight and would need to shower and dress. Time dragged.

Suddenly drums started up in the distance and then a rhythmic chanting joined in. There seemed to be no definite beat and yet at the identical moment the voices, both male and female, came in together on the same note. It had something primeval about it and tugged Debbie to her feet and out into her tiny garden, where the mosquitoes immediately began to bite. The sound was coming from the place where the path led through the trees, and going back for her torch Debbie put a scarf over her bare arms and decided to take a walk and look at what was going on.

She had only gone about a hundred yards, however, when the torch lit up a lurking, furry shape with two staring, red eyes. The torch fell from Debbie's nerveless hands and the thing growled as it scented her fear and panic. She scrabbled about for a moment seeking the torch and the eyes came nearer, and the growl sounded more menacing. Back through the trees she could see her house, and the lamp still shining through the window. She turned and ran, tripped and fell, picked herself up convinced that she would be torn to pieces at any moment and hurled herself through her gate, pausing to bolt it, and so into her living room.

By now she was whimpering like a gibbering idiot and practically incoherent. Determined she wouldn't sleep in that place for a single night, with that monster lurking outside, she took the lamp and left the house by the exit leading on to the tennis court, and ran towards the compound and Jim's bungalow, where she fell hysterically into his surprised arms. He was still wearing his white coat and had obviously just come off duty, but she clung and clung while he made soothing little noises and stroked her hair.

'Hey, love, what's up? Here, let me have that thing.' He took the lamp, which had flared up as she ran with it and blackened the glass with smoke and handed it to a third party, while she still sobbed into his shoulder. 'Now, come on! What's happened? Who's upset you?' He looked down at her. The pale green dress with its broderie anglaise was ripped and on it was blood from a cut on her knee. Her hair, such a short while ago satin-smooth, was now full of grass and twigs and there was a smudge of earth on her nose. 'You've had a tumble,' he said. 'What a sight you look!'

She thought, somewhat hysterically, that she had dressed up to please him and now he was criticising her appearance. Her whimpering changed to a kind of laughter and he shook her sharply.

'Now, Debbie, pull yourself together. None of that. Sit down and have a small whisky. Dawa! Small whisky and water for Missie. Now, for goodness' sake dry your eyes and tell me what you've been up to?'

She took the drink from the steward, who seemed to be trying not to notice anything was wrong—though goodness knew what he would have to say to the other stewards later—and took a gulping draught of it.

'I notice you ask what *I've* been up to, not what might have caused *me* trouble,' she complained tremulously.

'Darling, I haven't been able to get a word out of you till now. I want to hear why you've come to me looking as though you've been dragged through a bush backward. You *haven't* been dragged through a bush backward, have you?' he asked, his voice rising.

'Of course not. I——'

'Well, thank God for that! There's very little of that kind of assault goes on here, actually, and I should have thought you capable of taking care of yourself. Well——?' He sat opposite her, waiting.

'I was all ready and waiting when I heard the drums and the singing. I thought I'd go and see. I took a torch and—and then——'

'And then——?' he prompted.

'And then I saw this animal. Oh, it was so big and ferocious! Its eyes were red and it snarled. Jim, do they have black leopards here?'

'Black leopards? Whatever are you talking about? There've been no leopards hereabouts for ages. Occasionally in remote villages the leopard-men strike—they're a kind of secret society—but we're not as remote as that. The only thing that can hurt you hereabouts, Debbie, is a snake that you might tread on. There are still a few poisonous varieties about, but we have every known antidote in the hospital, so don't let that worry you, as snakes aren't lying in wait just to bite you. They're shy creatures, really, and will slither away given the chance.'

'I saw a big black animal with great red eyes.'

'Oh, come on, Debbie. You saw a dog taking a walk.'

She jumped up knocking over what remained of her whisky. The boy Dawa appeared and removed the empty glass.

'Don't tell me what I saw!' she shouted. 'I saw a big black animal and I could see its great teeth snarling at me before I dropped my torch and ran.'

Jim turned away as Dawa reappeared with a cloth and wiped the floor. The steward stood and asked, 'Missie want more whisky?'

'No, Missie doesn't,' Jim answered for her. 'I'll call you if I need you, Dawa. See to chop. Take Sister a tray over.'

'Yes, Doctor, sir.'

'Three bags full,' added a sullen Debbie. 'You've got him well trained, I must say. Perhaps, as I'm having delusions and seeing black leopards, I should go away and sleep it off, then you and Sister could have dinner together without any fuss or bother.'

Suddenly Jim was shaking her, but so mildly that her teeth didn't even rattle, and yet she knew he was as angry as he could get.

'I give up, Debbie,' he sighed, letting her go. 'All day I've had innuendoes from you of one sort or another and I simply don't understand you. Are you trying to quarrel with me? Do you want us to break things off? We will if it's what you want, Debbie.'

'I think it's better to do it this way than perhaps break up in bitterness and disillusionment at the end of my appointment here. I mean, we'll be working together, and I'll be seeing you at mealtimes and—and maybe we'll have a game of tennis together, some time? I'm not doing this very well, but I'd—I'd like to start getting to know you all over again. I'd like you not to think you have to kiss me because it's expected. Earlier today *I* was doing all the kissing and embarrassing you because you weren't quite ready. One day, I would hope, we'd suddenly know there was going to be a kiss and it would be—like the first time. Do you agree?'

'I want you to be happy, snub-nose.'

This was his intimate name for her and she smiled mistily.

'I never knew an engagement broken so amicably before,' she said.

'Let's call it a pause in our affairs,' he told her. 'Any good tactician pauses while he thinks about his next move. And it's not only a snub nose, it's muddy. We must get you cleaned up.'

There was a rattling of dishes in the kitchen, a dropping of cutlery.

'That's Dawa telling us dinner is more than ready to be served,' Jim smiled. 'My bedroom's down there and the bathroom's off. Do yourself up and be as quick as you can.' He was taking off his white coat. 'I won't bother showering until I'm ready to pop into bed. Hurry along, then. Use my things.'

Debbie saw herself in a long mirror and thought she'd never seen such a scarecrow. No wonder Jim had found it so easy to disengage himself! But it was odd how none of that really hurt. In fact she felt as though a load had been lifted from her mind. She was free now. Free to do her job and think about the future without expecting anything of Jim, but maybe finding the experience pleasant when he had something to offer.

She cleaned her face and hands, washed her bloody knee and found a plaster in Jim's bathroom cupboard to put over the scrape. She raked the grass and twigs out of her hair with Jim's comb and at last looked more like her old self. Only the tear in her dress remained. She went back to the main room where Dawa was already serving soup.

'Ah, good!' said Jim, getting to his feet and obviously approving. 'That's better. There you are, your old snub-nosed self again.'

'Tip-tilted, if you don't mind,' she said, trying to look down her nose, which was definitely on the short side. 'Gosh, but I'm hungry!'

'Do start. We've kept Dawa a bit, while we've been talking. When he's served the coffee he goes off to join his mates.'

'Couldn't I make the coffee and do the serving? You could let him go now.'

'No. That's not done out here. The stewards are jealous of their duties and don't like us showing our faces in the kitchen. He'll faithfully collect all our dirty dishes, except the coffee cups, which he'll expect us to leave here, and then leave the washing up till morning, and push off.'

'I don't seem to have a steward-boy yet.'

'No. Well, things were a bit rushed when it was definitely known you were coming. They threw up a house, and——'

'Yes, you live in considerably greater luxury than I

do. You can even walk all round your bed.'

'As I said, you're a novelty. We don't even know if you'll stay after six months, or be given the opportunity to do so. It all depends on results and the people at the top. So your accommodation may be a bit temporary at present . . .'

'It's downright primitive.' She saw that Jim was looking a bit unhappy as Dawa brought in the main course of roast guinea-fowl, and the green beans and sweet potatoes which are the stable vegetables of Africa. 'I'm not grumbling, but I would like a boy. I can't climb up and see to my shower, and even if I could, as you say, it's not done.'

'Right, I'll speak to the Director. He comes from Okusha and will know of some likely lad. You pay your steward yourself. Did you know that? The going rate is about thirty-five niaras a month—the equivalent of fifteen English pounds—but your boy would have less to do than either Dawa or Joseph or Shinja, who does for Saba and Iloro, so I would offer him twenty-five niaras. Eve and I pay Dawa fifty niaras for the two of us, because we usually share the same table. Eve trained Dawa and I think he's very good.'

Debbie found herself remembering Joseph, and how kind and attentive he had been. She doubted Dawa, who was somewhat sly-eyed, would have helped her at all, though no doubt she was prejudiced.

'That was delicious,' she said, as the steward came to remove the plates. Actually the fowl had been a bit stringy, but she was not yet used to African food and refused to complain for the sake of complaint. Portions of melon were brought in, red watermelon, fleshy, tasteless, but strangely wet and refreshing. 'We never settled about what I actually saw tonight, did we?' she asked with a nervous little laugh. 'I mean, if I see it again I'd like to know.'

'I think you saw the veterinary officer's dog, Debbie.'

'A dog? But——' she raised her hand four feet from the floor—'Jim, it was enormous! And—and fierce.'

'I know. It's a German shepherd, and a monstrous great handsome brute. Eve says they go together, him and it. What's it's name, now? Wolf, I think. Yes, Wolf.'

'It shouldn't be roaming loose,' Debbie complained. 'I was terrified.'

'You should never let an animal see you're frightened of it, Debbie. They can smell fear and it brings out the brute in them.'

'So Mr Roland doesn't live far from here?'

'About a mile or so. The path behind your house leads to a small Moslem village, and beyond that is the veterinary officer's bungalow. He's been to dinner at the hospital once since I arrived—we were all invited to the Director's bungalow for it—but I've never been out to his place. I must say I felt a bit antipathetic towards him, but that may have been because of what I'd heard about him, as Eve had seen a bit of him before I arrived out here. I don't suppose that's very fair of me to dislike a chap on somebody else's say-so.'

'And damme, Jim boy,' Debbie teased, 'but you're nothing if you're not fair. I suppose I really ought to call on him.'

'Whatever for?' Jim asked.

'Well, we did travel about seven hundred miles together, *and* I was in his company all last night, as Sister Meadows pointed out. In fact I was in his company for two nights. During the flight I made a nuisance of myself, falling all over him being sick. But I think I should at least say thank you. Otherwise I would still be at an airport hotel near Lagos.'

'Well, watch it, Debbie. I don't like running a chap down behind his back, but——'

'He's a devil with women, eh?'

'I don't really know. But there was a scandal—I know that. We're not the only Europeans here. There are tea and coffee planters, and estate managers, and the mine manager is white, and married, though it doesn't produce much nowadays—the mine, that is. The woman in the case went home and I believe there was a divorce. I don't know any details, I prefer not to.'

'But you really have pre-judged Jean-Marc Roland, in spite of your inherent fair-mindedness, haven't you, Jim? So far as you're concerned he was the guilty party in some divorce and so you don't want to know him socially. The woman in the case may have thrown herself at him, been bored out of her tiny mind in a place like this with her husband away, maybe for days at a time, and I shouldn't think there's much to do for women without jobs hereabouts. They're not allowed to do a stroke of work in their own houses, thanks to the steward-boys' union, and one can't knit or crochet for ever without going nuts. I should think to somebody like that Jean-Marc could look pretty attractive. In any case I shall call on him to say my piece and that is my only intention. Now, how do I get into Okusha? Can one borrow a car?'

'Well, we only take the hospital vehicles on official business. I've ordered a car from Arusha—a doctor is going home on extended furlough and assures me the Ford Cortina is in good fettle—but I haven't had the chance to collect it yet. Eve has her own small Austin. I borrow that, on occasions, but——'

'I don't want Sister to think I expect to beg and borrow from her. How far is it to Okusha?'

'About three and a half miles. But Europeans don't walk much hereabouts, and you'd be exhausted in no time, Debbie. What do you want in Okusha? Forgotten your toothbrush?' he joked.

'No. But I have got a week to fill in and there are odds and ends I need. It's going to seem a very long week. I must obviously think of buying an old banger for myself. What did you do while you were acclimatising yourself?'

'I spent every day in the hospital, watching and learning. I stood in at the Director's ops. I nearly passed out the first time, it was so damned hot under those lights in theatre. You can do the same. Watch and learn.'

'Sister's advised me not to.' Jim looked at her sharply. 'She says somebody would feel bound to attend to me and that I'd be better to enjoy my leave while I can and keep out of the way. I mean, just imagine if I upset the routine!'

'I'm sure Sister was thinking only of your good,' said Jim.

'Yes. Oh, I'm sure I'll find something to do. It's Saturday tomorrow, isn't it?'

'That's right. We Europeans are usually off duty from Saturday at noon until Monday a.m. We may attend church in Okusha on Sunday mornings, if we like, but the rest of the day we relax or play tennis or whatever. Eve and I had planned to take a trip up to Abama National Park this weekend, where the scenery is beautiful and there's a motel and swimming pool. That was before we got your telegram, of course. We were going in her car. I suppose you'd be automatically included, now, if you'd like to go.'

'Oh, no, Jim, I wouldn't think of it.'

'Very well, then, Debbie, what shall we do?'

She looked at him uncomprehendingly for a moment. 'Well, of course you and Sister must go as planned, Jim. I'm much too disorganised to go off on pleasure trips at the moment, and I don't want to go on any long car journeys until I've got over the last one. When I close my eyes I can still see that eternity of road flashing past my mind's eye. Jim, you're to do as you want to, do you hear? There are no strings between us now, and I'm sure you were looking forward to a swim. Who's in charge of the hospital at weekends, then?'

'Doctors Saba and Iloro, and the English wife of an Indian store owner in Okusha, who used to be a nurse, takes over and relieves Eve. In emergency the Director can always be reached. He lives in Okusha.'

'But I thought he lived right here,' said Debbie.

'So he does from Monday to Friday evening. Then he goes home to his wife and kids. She's a very humble woman—he married her when he'd just started at university—but she could never extend herself to fit in with the life his job offered. He loves her, in his way, but his job comes first. He has three sons, the eldest is now practising in Lagos and the other two are in London hospitals, but then he had a run of daughters and the youngest are about nine and ten. So he has this other home to go to at weekends; this other separate life. Odd, isn't it?'

'I think it's rather sweet,' said Debbie. 'Nice to think he hasn't grown away from his family.'

'Oh, and they're Christians,' Jim added. 'Staunch Catholics. Don't forget that.'

'I can't see myself getting into religious arguments with the hospital Director,' said Debbie. 'Anyway, being Christian isn't our prerogative, is it? I suppose there's an Anglican church, just in case I want to go some time?'

'We're well catered for as far as our souls go hereabouts. Anglican and Catholic, Moslem and Hindu, even a small synagogue. The missionaries did their job well.'

Shortly after this Debbie began to feel very sleepy. 'I think I'll go to bed now, Jim, if I can be sure that wasn't a black leopard I saw!'

'I can assure you of that, Debbie. Come on, I'll see you home. Here's your lamp all nicely cleaned up, but I'll lend you another torch seeing that you lost yours. So it is O.K. if I go off with Eve tomorrow?'

'You don't even have to ask. Of course it is. I'm going to have a long lie in, so in case I don't see you, have a good time.'

Jim saw her settled, the lamp and a tin of matches, in which they would keep dry, on the table and the borrowed torch beside her bed. He closed the louvred shutters on all the windows, told her to bolt the door after him and left.

She had thought she might not sleep, but was scarcely aware of tucking the mosquito net around her before she was deep in the arms of Morpheus.

CHAPTER FOUR

DEBBIE groaned a little as she awoke at length. She didn't really want to wake up at all, not for days and days, but a deep discomfort beset her too much to sleep on. She finally opened her eyes, looked about her and realised where she was and that both she and the bed-clothes were soaking wet with sweat. She sat up and flung off the mosquito net, which did manage to keep quite a lot of air out along with pests, and put her legs over the edge of the bed. She felt miserably dirty and aware that she would find only last night's slops in the shower-room and no fresh water in the tank above. It was then that she noticed on the tiny bedside table a steaming cup of tea and glanced up to question the fact that the louvred shutters were half open, though their hooked fastenings were on the inside of the room. She began to drink the tea before she asked herself further questions. It was good, hot and sweet, most refreshing. Maybe the sound of it being set down had wakened her up in the first place. But who could have done it? Was it the kindly Joseph, whose master spent his weekends in Okusha with his family?

Then she saw that the clothes she had stepped out of last night, too tired even to fold them, had disappeared. She couldn't hear a sound, though, and pulled on a towelling wrap to go and investigate. Firstly she saw her things, obviously freshly washed, hanging on a string stretched from her kitchen to the fence. It *must* be Joseph, bless him! Now she was fairly certain she'd find her shower attended to and, surely enough, when she pulled the chain fresh water came down and she was able to wash all the perspiration of the night away.

She began to sing as she towelled herself down and redonned her robe. Things might not be so bad after all. She saw that it was only half past eight and much earlier than she had intended rising, but she felt refreshed and alert. Going back into the bedroom to dress, she stared again. The bed had been stripped in her absence and even the mattress was draped over the windowsill to air. That Joseph certainly knew his stuff and she hoped she got a boy exactly like him. The mosquito net was tied neatly off overhead. Debbie opened her trunk and dressed, not in uniform today, but a pale blue poplin dress with a pleated skirt and white piping round the neck and sleeves. As she emerged into the living-room she smelled the heavenly fragrance of coffee and simply had to go and say good morning and thanks a lot to Joseph. A complete stranger regarded her somewhat fearfully: not a pyjama-clad stranger but a lad in ragged singlet and bleached khaki shorts.

'Hello!' said Debbie. 'Who are you?'

'Me steward-boy,' the lad said with a bow. 'Steward-boy. Got papers.' He thrust a well-thumbed booklet at her which she opened automatically at the first page where a startled-looking photograph of the lad stared back at her. Written opposite was the information that his name was Mohammed Kadiri, that he was a male, twenty-one years old, and lived in number two compound, Ekoto village in the Central Province. Opposite the place where his signature should have been was a blotched cross and a thumb-print.

'You can't write?' Debbie asked, uncomfortably.

'Can't write, but talk good. Can count money. Work very hard. Got letters, missie look!'

Debbie turned a page and saw indeed a letter written in Arabic. She turned another page and would guess that was written in either Pushtu or Tamil. She smiled questioningly at the boy.

'You haven't worked for a European before?'

He frowned in concentration and she realised she had to bring her English down to his level of understanding.

'You no work white people before?' she asked.

'No. But cleaning very same all over. Wash sheets and clo's every day, make bathroom ready, go shopping, cook food. Missie have food for brekfus somewhere?'

Debbie sniffed at the coffee still boiling and said, 'I don't think I have.'

'That O.K., missie. I get.'

'But, Mohammed——'

'Mohammed is all boys' name,' he told her. 'My special name Kadiri.'

'Well, Kadiri, this is only a small house and I can only offer you twenty-five niaras a month. How's that?'

'No, no!' the other said, quite severely. 'Not pay anything one whole month. Kadiri need experience working for white people. Kadiri not like working Injun people. Kadiri work for twenty niaras, right job. Now Missie go and Kadiri fetch brekfus.'

'How did you get in?' Debbie asked as she was turning away.

'Oh, very easy, know how,' and Kadiri smiled deprecatingly. 'Kadiri put bolts on winder keep other peoples out. Now Missie go.'

'Well, the Director remembered all the time,' Debbie thought as she went back to her sitting-room.

'He must have sent the boy and he seems very efficient. But poor—his singlet has been mended and mended until it won't hold together, but he smells clean.'

Kadiri eventually reappeared, quite out of breath as though he had been running, and laid the table with the only cup and saucer she had, and a white plate she hadn't seen before. He set down the coffee in a brass jug—funny, she didn't know she had a brass jug—and then from a folded leaf served a helping of boiled rice sprinkled with fresh apricots and groundnuts. There was a small earthenware jug of milk and she guessed it came from a goat as she put it in her coffee and it was so obviously very creamy. She enjoyed her breakfast, and said so when Kadiri came to remove the dishes.

She supposed Jim and Sister would have left by now for their weekend's leisure, and wondered what to do with herself. At that moment she heard an altercation in her backyard which bordered the tennis court and heard the unmistakable dark brown tones of the hospital Director, followed by younger men's voices in sharp argument. She rushed outside and the Director held out his big brown orthopaedist's hand in greeting. He was accompanied by two little girls in European-type cotton dresses. Both had stubble hair dressed in dozens of tiny plaits. One was in pink and the other wore yellow. They were amiably plain children but smiled uninhibitedly. The elder one had large, permanent teeth protruding, but the smaller girl had tiny, even milk teeth, gloriously free of decay.

'Good morning, sir—girls,' said Debbie. 'I thought you were off at weekends.'

'So I am. My daughters Patricia and Theresa.' The children bobbed little curtseys. Sweet, thought Debbie.

Joseph appeared suddenly from the kitchen bundling Kadiri in front of him. Joseph was a big lad and had the other held firmly with one arm behind his back and his own strong right arm half throttling his prisoner.

'Oh, please let him go, Joseph!' Debbie pleaded.

The Director said something in Yoruba and Joseph released the squirming Kadiri, who hung his head against the splendour of a steward in a smart green starched pyjama suit.

'Where did you get *him*?' asked Dr Oduloru.

'He's my steward-boy. He was here when I awoke. I thought you'd sent him.'

'I know nothing about him. In fact that's what I came to see you about. Joseph was going to see to you for today while I looked around town for a suitable boy.'

'He seems very good,' Debbie said. 'I've had a lovely breakfast and he's done my washing and seen to the shower. What's wrong with him?'

'Well, we don't know anything about him, do we? You realise he's a Moslem?'

'I hadn't thought about it, but of course, with a name like Mohammed he must be. But is that important, sir? I mean, we all worship the same God in our own way.'

Dr Oduloru smiled fractionally and then addressed Kadiri in Yoruba. The lad produced his work book and the Director perused its contents. He seemed to be quite a linguist, because he had no difficulty with the two letters.

'The first reference, from an Egyptian family, speaks very highly of the boy, saying he is industrious and polite. The second, however, accuses him of being a thief. He probably doesn't know that he is carrying round evidence against himself, because he can't read. He has told me he has had no work for five months and heard you were in need of a steward-boy and so tried to get in first. I'm going to tell him what the letter says.'

Debbie watched absolute horror spread over

Kadiri's countenance as the Director translated the contents of the letter for his benefit. A knowing smile curled Joseph's lip. There was a kind of dignity about Kadiri as he spoke to Dr Oduloru, and tears of outrage in his eyes.

'He says,' explained the Director, 'that he worked for an Indian family for only twenty niaras a month, which is not the going rate, I may tell you. For perks he was supposed to get four packets of cigarettes a month and a bar of soap. One month he didn't get either cigarettes, or soap, and didn't complain, then the family had visitors from Lagos, which meant the lad had to do for eight adults and five children. The second month he didn't get his perks, he mentioned them, and his employer told him that steward-boys were two a penny or one a kobo, whichever you prefer, and he could forget about such things in future. So that week he helped himself to a bar of soap and decided to leave, without claiming any wages. To get another job he had to have a reference from his last employer, so he went back, and the rest you know. That's if the boy's to be believed, of course.'

Joseph said something in dialect and Kadiri flew at him. The Director intervened and obviously sharply reprimanded his own steward.

'He called him a dirty Muslim pig,' he told Debbie. 'I told him we don't want a religious war.'

Debbie was now aware of a small blue-clad figure behind Kadiri. She had the inevitable brass pot on her head and the two Oduloru girls eyed her curiously.

'My brother is not a thief,' she declared ringingly. 'He took only his own soap. People should not break promises.'

'So that's how Kadiri heard about the job,' said Debbie. 'This is my friend; we meet at the tap. Her name's Dina.'

'And what about her brother?' asked the Director. 'That is really the sixty-four-thousand-dollar question, eh? Does he go or stay?'

'He offered to work for a month for nothing,' Debbie said. 'I shan't hold him to that, but as far as I'm concerned he stays. Is—is that all right with you, sir?'

'Let's show the Christian spirit and give him a chance, eh? Joseph——' he spoke sharply to his own steward in Yoruba, who protested but was shouted down. Joseph then wandered off.

The Director accompanied Debbie and Kadiri around her premises on a tour of inspection, and he finally handed her a list. 'These you can get in Okusha town, charged to the hospital. They're necessities for your house and will be known as fixtures and fittings. Pretty china and food you will pay for yourself. Have you changed any money?'

'No, I——'

'Well, the banks are closed today, but here are two hundred niaras to put you on. Your boy will need uniform, so you'd better take him to a tailor's. If he's worth his salt he'll know where to go. I've told Joseph to lend him some things, meanwhile, and here he is.'

Joseph handed over a green pyjama suit and a white one with brass buttons. His brow was still lowering with resentment.

'Thank you very much, Joseph,' Debbie said, 'for your help yesterday, and your willingness to help me today. I'm very grateful.'

The Director said something sharp and pointed.

The steward at last smiled awkwardly. 'My master say no good being Christian if behave like heathen. O.K. by me.' He held out his hand to Kadiri, who shook it readily, grinning the while.

'Now we're going into Okusha,' the Director said, 'when your boy has changed and is fit to be seen. You'd like to do some shopping, wouldn't you?'

'That would be very nice,' Debbie smiled, and held up the money, 'and this makes it possible, thank you, sir.'

'You can drop me off at my house and Sunday, my

chauffeur, will then be at your disposal with the Land-
Rover. Don't rush things, but the main stores do close
at one on Saturdays.'

After shopping Kadiri suggested she go for a walk
while he cleaned the house.

'Very well. I go see Master Roland, the vet man.
You know him?'

'Master with big dog?' Kadiri smiled. 'Yes, know
him. He make all dog, cat, goat and cow have medicine so they not get sick. Animal more better than
people,' and he laughed at his own joke. 'He live
through my village, then some way down road. Big
house. Big dog.'

'I know,' Debbie said ruefully, and when she had
carefully brushed her hair and freshened herself up she
set out once more through the trees.

It was three o'clock and still very hot. She wondered
how she would ever be able to do her job in this climate, but told herself that she had only arrived yesterday
from the November chill of Britain and that her blood
was still thick. She had taken a salt tablet with her tea,
but had no sooner entered the claustrophobic atmo-
sphere of the trees, which seemed to exude humidity,
than she felt her temples throbbing. She walked slowly,
looking up at the brilliant blossoms of flame of the
forest and blue jacaranda, picked up a trumpet-shaped
blossom only to throw it away with a shudder, alive as
it was with insects. She came to the village where
Kadiri and Dina must live, but it was silent at this
hour. A toddler trotted out of one of the houses and its
mother called sleepily after it, and when it saw a
strange white face it ran back, crying. A village dog
barked, but only desultorily, and then continued to
scratch itself. One building, with a kind of tower to it,
must be the mosque. The door to it was open and a
multi-coloured carpet lay within.

Debbie knew she was nearing the road when a
mammy-wagon went past loaded with humanity and

their purchases from the town. She was tired and hot and uncomfortable when a big bungalow came into view standing in a large compound. She might as well go and pay her respects now, hoping for a lift back. She saw the Land-Rover and a big Mercedes standing in a garage so it looked as though he was home. She struggled with a gate and carefully shut it behind her, and then—oh, lord—the creature came from regions behind the house and straight at her. Forgetting what Jim had said about a dog being able to smell fear, she turned and ran, came up against a strong fence and turned at bay.

The dog was huge, the biggest shepherd she had ever seen. It had powerful shoulders and hindquarters and was all black apart from one flash of beige on one pricked ear. Its eyes were bright and menacing and as she bit her lip it lifted its own in a snarl.

'Wolf!' called a voice from the house. Debbie had never been so glad to see anyone in her life. 'Where are your manners?' He came striding across the compound. 'Bad dog! Say you're sorry!'

Now the great dog was lying on its back waving all four legs in the air. Across the writhing, furry body Jean-Marc Roland said, 'Hello, Miss Wyndham. Settling in?'

'I think so. I—I didn't thank you for all your trouble. You just shot off.'

'Then come on in and do it properly in the shade.'

As Debbie took a step the dog was again on its feet and snarling.

'I think I'd better introduce you two,' said Jean-Marc. 'You scared of dogs, or something? He seems to think so.'

'He and I met last night in the dark. I was petrified. With your talk of leopards I thought I'd found one.'

'Well, he's not a leopard, as you see, but he can be a bully if you let him. Now address him by name, quietly, and look him in the eye, then lift your hand very slowly and let him sniff it.'

Somehow Debbie managed to comply though her heart was palpitating.

'Friend,' Jean-Marc said to the animal. 'Good dog! Now clear off.'

Debbie thought, 'Well, I've made friends with one of them, at least. It may not be quite so easy with the master.'

She told herself it was imagination which made her think the brilliant blue eyes had lit up on seeing her. It must be. He must have seen, and surely have loved, so many women in his time.

Debbie looked appreciatively around the well-furnished sitting-room and sipped her iced tea, with its slice of lemon, through a straw. The furniture was mostly of rattan, plaited cane and painted white, which was cool to sit on, though there was a solid-looking coffee-table made from a single plank of some dark red wood, beautifully grained and polished, and matching bookcases lining two walls of the room. Debbie looked longingly at the books and walked over to study them. Books made a residence look so permanent, so like home, in that they reflected the occupier's tastes and personality. Some were German classics, she saw the titles of Schiller and Goethe, and then there were French masters of the written word, Zola, Anatole France, Rousseau; Shakespeare headed the English list, his complete works, followed by Dickens and Boswell's life of Dr Johnson.

Jean-Marc re-entered the room—he had been called out by a steward—and his brilliant eyes gleamed on his bookshelves.

'The staff of my life,' he said. 'Much more than is bread. All the moderns are over there, if you'd like to borrow anything. Apart from the bottom shelf where I keep my professional textbooks in the oiled-cloth wraps. Everything has to be protected here, or the termites would grow too fat. Where are your car keys? My boy will bring your vehicle inside. The road isn't very wide just here.'

'I haven't a car,' she said, sitting down again.

'Oh. Somebody dropped you off, then? Where are you being picked up?'

'I walked here. Nobody's picking me up. But don't worry——'

'You *walked* here? Your fiancé allowed that?'

'Oh, he doesn't know about it. He's gone away for the weekend.'

'Gone away——?' Jean-Marc seemed to recollect himself and went to speak to the waiting steward. He returned to say, 'It's very easy to get heat-stroke, you know. Nobody's immune. You're supposed to take things very easily for at least a week.'

'I'm sorry, I always seem to behave in your sight like an extremely wayward and naughty child. I know all about the risks. When it was decided I was to come I was advised to sail out, which gives one twelve days in which to become acclimatised. But I was so anxious, at that time, to see Jim that I insisted on flying, and I *was* warned to take things very easily for a week. It's just that you don't think anything can happen to you personally, and it didn't seem a bad idea to come and say thank you. After all, it wasn't a long walk, and—and here I am.'

'Yes, as you say, here you are.' Their eyes met and Debbie turned hers away quickly. 'I'm very glad to see you, Miss Wyndham, but you *will not* be walking back to the hospital. I will take you when you want to go. I'm puzzled about one thing, if you wouldn't consider it an impertinence——?'

'What's that?' she smiled encouragingly.

'You were so anxious to see your fiancé that you simply had to fly out, and yet you say he's gone away for the weekend and—and left you?'

'Oh, well, it was all arranged and he naturally

expected me to go along. But I refused and he offered to stay with me. That seemed silly, so—so they went and I stayed. I had to unpack and—and so forth. Anyway——' her voice sounded thin and high in her own ears—'he isn't my fiancé any more.'

'Oh, Miss Wyndham, I'm sorry. I'm very sorry. I—I don't know what to say.'

'Oh, good gracious! What is there to say?'

'Well, you must realise Africa is a strange place. It has a sort of pervasive magic about it. It changes people and situations so that they are not entirely real any more. It lends a kind of enchantment to situations which are not normal. Most often these things don't last and then people become their old selves again. I wouldn't be too unhappy if I were you.'

'Unhappy?' Debbie echoed. 'What have I to be unhappy about?'

'I'm sorry, I must have misunderstood. Usually when an engagement is broken somebody is unhappy.'

'Well, it isn't me. And anyway,' Debbie was on her dignity now, and had risen, 'I don't know what we're talking about my affairs for. I'm sure you have lots of other interests and things you should be doing, so I'll be going. Don't worry about me. I'll be perfectly all right.'

Outside, in the compound, however, Wolf waited and crouched in front of her. When she tried to walk round him he was as nimble as a cat and snarled.

'Would you,' she called over her shoulder, 'please call your dog off?'

'I'm not sure I should,' said Jean-Marc. 'He knows you ladies shouldn't be out without hats and he can scent your hostility.'

'Call him off!' she shouted, as Wolf showed a full set of excellent teeth at her.

'No. Come back inside, simmer down and I'll send you home in the Land-Rover. Festus can drive you if my presence is suddenly anathema.'

Debbie climbed back up the steps and Wolf went to his place under the house.

'Sorry if I was touchy,' she said to the wall of books in front of her. 'I shouldn't take things out on you. You've only shown me consideration if—if not exactly kindness. But that dog of yours is a menace. Would he really have attacked me if I'd tried to pass him?'

'I should always keep on the right side of him, and of me,' Jean-Marc smiled, 'and then we may never have to find that out.'

A boy appeared with a tea-tray containing the refreshing beverage and a plate of thin tomato sandwiches and a kind of coconut cake.

'Cookie ask is Missie staying to dinner?' he inquired as he set the tray down on the table.

'Well, are you?' asked Jean-Marc.

'Oh, look, I don't want to impose. Don't misunderstand me, Mr Roland, but I should feel that you thought I'd angled all this. I came just to say thanks, and—and have a look at the scenery. I've practically told you I'm alone this weekend and you ask me to dinner. Now, what would you say in my place?'

'I'd say tell Cookie two for dinner,' Jean-Marc nodded at the boy, who smiled and disappeared. 'Now, shall I pour or will you do it?' Debbie lifted up the tea-pot without more ado. 'I've stopped analysing events or presuming that two and two will automatically make four any more. The best laid plans, with me, inevitably gang agley, so I play things as they come. Today I was planning a quiet evening, a few records, and you arrive out of the blue and I'm not even arguing. Why are you?'

'Because I'm afraid of people thinking I'm chasing you, I suppose.'

'And are you?'

'Good heavens, what a thing to say!'

'You said it, not I.'

'I came out to be with Jim, not to pick up with any

Tom, Dick or Harry who might be around!'

'But you're not with Jim, are you?'

'No, but we haven't had a row or anything. That's quite true. There's been nothing.'

'Except a broken engagement.'

'Well, not broken, exactly. Sort of deferred. We're both free, but there's an understanding between us.'

'Has Jim been unfaithful to you?'

Debbie smiled wryly. 'Oh, no, not Jim. He's almost painfully loyal. He—wouldn't. Not while he was engaged to me.'

'But now he's free, you say.'

'Do you want me to think he's making passionate love to Sister Meadows at this moment?' and Debbie smiled despite herself.

'Oh, so that's who he's with. No, this isn't the hour for lovemaking. It's still far too hot, *and* broad daylight.'

'Is that the voice of experience speaking?' Debbie asked. Her cup rattled as she set it down in the saucer and then her lips parted in sudden laughter. 'Sorry!' she said quickly.

'You're not sorry at all,' he told her, putting forward his cup for a refill, 'and I'm not going to tell you. Fair enough?'

'Fair enough,' she smiled, 'for an unplanned meeting I think we're managing to say far too much, don't you?'

Somehow she found him so easy to talk to that she talked and talked, and he was a very good listener. Occasionally he paused to smoke half a pipeful of fragrant tobacco, especially after darkness fell and mosquitoes and other pests invaded the house.

'You've taken your proquanil?' he asked once.

'Yes. *And* my salt tablet. I shouldn't need those for much longer. Why is Wolf howling? He really sounds like one—a wolf, I mean.'

'There's a full moon and it seems to make his blood stir. Also it's time for his walk. Would you care for a moonlight walk?'

She hesitated only for a moment. 'Why not?' she asked.

He insisted on her draping a cardigan round her shoulders. It was one of his and big on her. It had a sort of masculine fragrance about it. She laughed up at him and noticed how his eyes could change almost to navy blue in the half light of the veranda. He took her arm to help her down the wooden steps and Wolf was promptly all over his master, jumping up, being pushed away, jumping up and being thrust away even harder. Then, 'Down, boy! It's O.K., we're going. No need for a whole circus act.'

The moon was an incredible silver disc in the sky and wore a sort of diaphanous outer garment.

'That's caused by the harmattan,' Jean-Marc explained. 'Thousands of particles of Saharan dust are carried south in this wind from the north, which has become a mere breeze by the time it reaches us. But it's a cold wind, probably originating in the High Atlas, and at night one can feel the chill, though one will still be sweating. The humidity is not affected. That is why one must always take care against chills.'

They were walking down a well-trodden path by the light of a torch Jean-Marc carried. He suddenly snapped it off, saying, 'It's like a glow-worm trying to compete with that moon. What's up?' Debbie had stopped and was peering around her.

'That scent. What is it?'

'Oh, the wild jasmine. Such an unassuming-looking little plant, but so fragrant. The locals believe it's an aphrodisiac. They come in pairs to sniff and then go and—or so I believe. But then, throughout time, people have believed in aphrodisiacs when it only takes the right people, paired at the right time. Am I offending you?'

A whiff of fragrant tobacco drowned the jasmine momentarily. Smells were a part of sensuality, she thought. 'No, of course you're not offending me,' she told him. 'I think such things are extremely interesting.' They plunged into the darkness of trees and she could hear the lapping of water, so they were somewhere near a river or a stream. 'Any snakes hereabouts?' she asked him.

'Wolf will tell us if there are. Don't be afraid. Hold my hand. I know this way blindfold, but of course you're new here.'

She reached out and drew strength and confidence from that strong grip.

'Go on about you and Jim,' he encouraged. 'You were feeling rejected by his reception of you. What did you expect, exactly?'

'Well, a long separation makes one forget things. I had forgotten the physical side of our relationship. I know sex isn't the be-all and end-all of an affair, but it has a certain importance in view of the fact that one has promised to marry someone. I knew that Jim was nice, and that he was terribly sincere and that once there had been some magic which had made me say yes when he proposed to me. That was the Jim I had forgotten and knew I had to find again. I even—I feel terribly ashamed of it—I even imagined I was just feeling terribly repressed, and at my goodbye party I allowed myself to be taken away by somebody else and we had quite a petting party. That man tried to persuade me not to come out here, but I knew quite well by that time that I wanted all that from Jim, and the other qualities which I hadn't forgotten in my fiancé. I knew Jim would never just use a woman for a cheap thrill, he'd have to be heart and soul in any enterprise before he would submit his body.

'So when I arrived I just wanted to assuage the appetite this other man had stirred in me with Jim, but it was in. I found myself trying to pick rows with him, it. I threw myself at him at the first opportunity and it's as though I was knocking at a door and nobody was in. I found myself trying to pick rows with him, but he spotted that and refused to be drawn. I expect it was my pride made me give him his ring back. I don't think he quite knows how to deal with me. Naturally my womanhood requires that I should have a special relationship with my fiancé, not that I be treated like a sister. If there's going to be nothing between us then I'd rather we were both free.'

'I wonder if you really do feel free? If Jim was, at this moment, feeling attracted strongly to some other woman, wouldn't you mind just a bit?'

'I don't know. I haven't thought about it. Yes, I suppose I would mind. She would have succeeded in stirring him where I had failed.'

'And how do you regard your own freedom? Do you want to be attracted to someone else? Or is it that you want Jim to feel he has to win you all over again by rediscovering the magic which turned you both on?'

'Hypothetical questions! How can one answer them? I'm playing things by ear at the moment. As you said a little while ago, two and two don't necessarily make four for me any more. Things may gang agley that I don't expect. But the only thing I can't bear is to find the biscuit box empty when I'm hungry—and that's the way it felt.'

'Do you notice anything?' They had stopped in a sort of amphitheatre which was almost a perfect circle. Above, the moon sailed, eyes, which were now known to be dried-up seas, looked down as humans look upon ants, and a smiling mouth, the biggest sea of all, held a kind of benignity. Though man had explored the bright side of the moon, the expression was still one of impassivity and untouchability.

'Should I?' Debbie asked, trying not to feel nervous.

'You are standing in a magic circle, no less, and should be touched by the enchantment. This is the vale of the moonflowers, as they are locally known, though they have an almost unpronounceable botanical name, and on a night such as this, with the moon at full, after the first spring rains they will bloom, a white carpet of them, more fragrant than the violets to which they are distantly related, and on that special night, if you are here to see, you will be granted three wishes.'

'You're making it all up,' Debbie accused.

'Oh, no, I'm not. About the three wishes, yes, maybe. But not about the moonflowers. They bloom for just one night. Don't you think that's magic in itself? Somewhere underneath our feet their roots are lurking and preparing for this annual event, a sort of nocturnal ballet, but if I switch on the torch you can see nothing, only that no grass grows here. Of course a deal of legend is woven around this elusive plant. Simeon tells me he came by here one night about his business, and there they were. He was so moved by the sight that he picked a bunch of the flowers—they have very short stems—and took them to his bungalow where he put them carefully into water. In the morning, however, they were quite dead and lifeless; only the water in the glass was red. They are said to bleed, you see. Someone else who picked one for his wild-flower collection found only a red stain next day. No flower at all.'

'Have you seen them?' Debbie asked.

'No. I've always been out of the district when they've bloomed. Maybe you'll be luckier. They are said to be especially kind to lovers, blessing their union. So round about April things will perhaps seem far different between you and Jim and he may bring you here.'

'It's a lovely story, anyway,' Debbie said, her face upturned still to his.

'You know,' he mused, 'you could be a moonflower blooming out of season. Is your hair really that colour? I mean girls can ring the changes, nowadays, quite literally. Maybe I shouldn't have asked.'

'Oh, that's all right. Yes, I'm naturally blonde. But I have inherited my father's brown eyes. My sister is a blue-eyed blonde, and——'

She could scarcely believe that his fingers were in her hair, gently running through it and then clutching suddenly and painfully so that she tensed involuntarily and gasped and opened her mouth to protest. His lips descended as surprisingly and somehow she was removed from herself, a disembodied spirit hovering and watching a fair-haired girl in an enchanted glade being kissed by a man who was practically a total stranger, and yet somehow as well known and predictable as time itself.

She at last made a few little noises and pushed him away. For a whole minute there was total silence and then he spoke, a trace of uncertain laughter in his voice.

'If you slap me, as is your prerogative, I shall promise not to set my dog on you.'

Debbie said, dully, somehow not really appreciating what had just happened, 'Don't worry. I'm not going to slap you. I think I ought to warn you that I've heard about you. You apparently have quite a reputation hereabouts.'

'Time to leave Fairyland,' he said sharply, calling Wolf to heel. 'Come on! Don't worry that I'll assault you again. Even with *my* reputation you're quite, quite safe.'

She had almost to run to keep up with him on the way back. As they arrived in the compound of the bungalow she asked, 'Would you like me to go home now? Obviously I've made you angry, which seems to be the story of our brief acquaintance. We'll cry enough, shall we, while we're quits?'

'No,' he told her consideringly, 'I don't think we'll cry enough. Explaining to Cookie would be too difficult, anyway, as I think he was killing our best-laying chicken especially to please you. I'm not angry with you, anyway. It's the people who spread the tittle-tattle who make me angry.'

It was by now nine o'clock and she was ravenous. They sat at a nicely-laid table and the boy, Simeon, served them a kind of lentil soup, with freshly-baked rolls. After this came the chicken, small by British standards but very plump. It was stuffed with sweetcorn and its own chopped liver and heart. With it were served the inevitable green beans and a salad.

'I suppose you're expecting me to enlarge on my "sins"?' Jean-Marc asked her, with one of those sudden devastating looks of his.

'Not unless you want to,' she said uncomfortably. 'I've rather used you as a confidant, but that doesn't mean——'

'I think it does,' he said thoughtfully. 'I may say that what happened back there was entirely spontaneous and—but that's not what you thought, is it? You thought, "Ah, with his reputation I might have known he'd make a pass at me." '

'No, I didn't. I didn't think you'd do—er—that. But I thought we might be friends.'

'You know, I didn't think I'd do that either? I was even working out how to get you back on the right terms with your Jim again, not nibble at the goodies myself. I can only apologise and put it down to that damned moon out there.'

'I don't think——' said Debbie—'that when a woman has been kissed, whether by accident or design, the situation is helped by an apology, exactly.' She looked a long time at her plate, and then was somehow magnetised into meeting Jean-Marc's gaze.

'I think I understand,' he told her. 'A woman would prefer to know the reaction of her partner in the enterprise. We-ll-' he drew out the word as Simeon collected the dirty plates and disappeared into the kitchen with them—'very nice. A little shy, a lot of promise. Jim must have put his emotions in formaldehyde by mistake. I think, in his shoes, I would want to do an awful lot of kissing. But I'm not, am I? You were looking to me for friendship and I trespassed. Also I have this reputation you've heard of. Well, I don't think I'm a dog with such a bad name, really. I'm a bachelor and there are lonely, bored and, sometimes, neglected wives in the district. Sufficient to say that only one, and I'm naming no names, has accused me on that score, and that after she'd left Nigeria her husband was still my friend and came to apologise for her public outburst. You know what they say about a woman scorned . . .?'

Simeon brought in fresh fruit cocktails and there was a delicious aroma of coffee from the kitchen.

'You must have had love affairs, though?' Debbie asked, and then blushed. 'Oh, how impertinent of me! Forget I asked that question, please.'

'No, why should I? Yes, I've been in love. At twenty, and twenty-one, a big affair when I was twenty-four. Oh, that was very painful.'

'Why?' Debbie asked.

'Well, I was coming out here and there had to be a parting. I suppose it was similar to you and Jim, really, though we weren't really engaged. Do you know we have a very civilised approach to sex in Switzerland? When a couple get engaged they are allowed to sleep together, without any eyebrows being raised, and if the girl becomes pregnant then they marry perhaps earlier than anticipated. But Pascale and I were not engaged and so there was nothing like that. After a year I returned home, so desperately in love that I had the engagement ring all ready, and a stranger looked back at me. I couldn't even embrace her. Yes, indeed, that was painful at the time. But one survives. Come on out on to the veranda for coffee.'

'It was a lovely meal and I'd like to thank your cook.'

'He shall be told. By the way, I can't keep calling a

girl I've kissed Miss Wyndham, can I?'

'Then try Debbie.'

'Very well, Debbie. I answer to Marc. The Jean part is my patronym. Nearly all boys are Jean something or other—Jean-Paul, Jean-Claud, Jean-Pierre. Now what can be done to ensure that you and Jim don't suffer the fate of Pascale and Marc, eh? You do want to get back to square one with him, don't you?'

'Of course.'

'Well, let me think about it. How about me sending a car for you tomorrow morning and coming with me for a jaunt round my territory? We'll have a light lunch and I'll get you back to the hospital for siesta. Your weekenders should be back soon after. And I wouldn't make a habit of allowing Jim to slip off with Sister Meadows. If even she allowed the ice to melt she could present some formidable competition.'

'I'll remember your words of warning,' Debbie smiled.

CHAPTER FIVE

DEBBIE enjoyed waking up in her soggy bed on this morning, knowing that her shower would be ready and waiting, for Kadiri had tapped on her door on this occasion and there was a delicious cup of tea for her to drink and her mosquito net lifted away.

When she had breakfasted Kadiri approached her excitedly saying that Master Roland's boy had come for her and that she was to wear trousers.

'Trousers?' Debbie asked. 'I wonder why?'

She could hear the two boys chatting as she dug into her trunk and pulled out a pair of faded blue jeans. She really didn't know why she had packed them unless it was with a thought to doing jobs around the house if she and Jim decided to get married. With them she wore a blue cotton long-sleeved blouse and so went outside where Kadiri, in his green pyjama suit, looked at her with a smile and the young man with him in frank curiosity.

'I am Festus, missie. I am mechanic, look after cars for Mr Roland. Sometimes I chauffeur.'

'Hello, Festus. I'll be away until siesta time, Kadiri. What are you going to do today?'

'After washing dry, I iron. Then I tell this man got to make Missie a garden. I get shubble and dig.'

'Good!' Debbie had no fears that her new 'boy' would idle his time away. Last night he had been awaiting her, late as it was, and had made her a cup of cocoa. The small house was gleaming and smelled of polish and insect-spray. He had asked for the back-door key, which connected with the open-ended kitchen, having secured new bolts to all the louvred windows.

In ten minutes the Land-Rover arrived in the compound of Jean-Marc Roland's bungalow, and he leapt down from the veranda to greet her.

'Have a good night?' he asked. 'Come and meet Mary Tate. She and I often breakfast together and I'm sure you can manage another cup of coffee.'

Debbie was introduced to a somewhat diminutive female who could have been anything from twenty-three to thirty. She was pretty in an elfin way, with a heart-shaped face and short brown curls. She wore a simple white linen dress which suited her, and her legs were bare and very brown, her feet in sandals.

'Mary's a teacher of the three R's in the local secondary school in Okusha,' Marc enlarged after the introductions, 'though she's really a very erudite young lady with a Cambridge honours degree and a Ph.D. in African studies. She would never tell you that herself.'

'Oh, Marc!' Mary Tate protested. 'You put people right off me from the start. Miss Wyndham will think

I'm a real bluestocking.'

Debbie was just wondering if Mary was one of the lonely, neglected wives of Okusha district when the other provided the necessary information.

'I was born out here, Miss Wyndham. My parents were both teachers in Ibadan. My father was Professor Tate; he translated various textbooks into Ibo and Yoruba so that the languages would not be lost. Unfortunately, in a way, English has been accepted as the standard language of education. There are, of course, so many peoples and languages and dialects in such a vast country that they could be divisive. Much the same thing happened in India where the only common language was the English of the Raj.'

'I'll leave you ladies gossiping while I get into my riding togs,' Marc said, rising from the table. 'You're going to get up on a horse again,' he told Debbie. 'It's much the best way of getting around.'

Debbie looked somewhat apprehensive. 'It's ages since I rode,' she said, 'and then only quiet school hacks.'

'You never forget,' he told her, 'like riding a bicycle.'

Mary Tate laughed when he had gone, and with the ease of apparent familiarity poured herself another cup of coffee.

'Quite a lad, our Marc, isn't he?' she asked. 'He's done wonders hereabouts.'

'I only arrived the day before yesterday,' Debbie said.

'Yes, I know. Marc was telling me how he brought you here to join your fiancé.'

She didn't say ex-fiancé, Debbie thought, so he hasn't told her about *that*.

'It's a pity that European members of the hospital don't mix with the rest of us,' Mary went on. 'We have a club in Okusha, with a swimming pool, badminton, all sorts of indoor games, a bar, the lot. But although Dr Oduloru looks in occasionally, and enjoys having a beer while his children swim, and Dr Saba is extremely popular with everybody, your fiancé and Sister Meadows keep themselves to themselves. But maybe you can change all that, eh?'

'I can try,' said Debbie. 'I know Jim is still studying hard. I think he wants to specialise, eventually, in tropical medicine.'

'Still, all work and no play, eh? I should know. I worked until I was a walking encyclopaedia and woke up to the fact, one day, that I wasn't really living at all. Now I hope I've got my priorities right.'

Debbie wondered what they were. Marriage, perhaps? A husband—Marc?

As Mary looked at her as though inviting a question, she asked, 'What's this nonsense about the moon-flowers? Is Marc a leg-puller?'

'Oh, no. You walked by the river last night, did you? They only grow in a few isolated areas nowadays, because who wants to leave land lying twelve months for a species which blooms on only one night of the year? Of course they're not true moonflowers, you know. The locals only call them that because of the time they choose to flower. I'll bet you didn't know that the common ox-eye daisy, in Britain, is also known as the moonflower?'

'No, I didn't,' Debbie said.

'Well, those hereabouts are not related to daisies. I believe they're very exotic and the scent is unbeliev-able.'

'So you haven't seen them?' Debbie asked.

'No. It can be a night of full moon and still be cloudy, you know,' said Mary Tate, 'and one's inclined to forget about them if one's busy about other things.'

Marc reappeared wearing jodhpurs and said, 'End of hen-party. Break it up, girls. I'm dining with you on Wednesday, Mary. True?'

'True. I shall cook you a curry. Don't be late.'

Marc walked with her to her car, which Festus had been diligently polishing. Debbie deliberately didn't watch the leavetaking. When he returned he said, 'Nice, isn't she? The nicest person I know. Come on and meet another lady, the one you're to ride. Don't worry, she's gentle and sober.'

They walked round the bungalow and in an inner courtyard Simeon was holding the heads of two horses. One was giving him no trouble; she was Klara, a middle-aged mare, but the other, a stallion, Fullani, was trying to bite the steward's hand through his bit. Marc gave him a reminding slap, helped Debbie to mount and then relieved Simeon of responsibility by taking control of his own horse.

Just for a moment Debbie panicked as Klara began to roll in a walking motion beneath her, and then memories of her riding lessons came back to her and she gripped with her knees, held the reins firmly but without tugging and glanced at her companion. They walked across the road and into the shade of trees. Insects buzzed, birds swooped and chirped and one yodelled in its yellow throat. The path widened and Marc asked, 'Could you manage a trot? My beast is raring to go.'

'I'll try,' said Debbie. She pressed with her knees and released her hold on the reins a fraction. Klara's body changed rhythm as she broke into a steady trot and still Debbie sat firm. She felt rather proud of herself. If only that was Jim riding away from her at a full gallop, obviously intending to give the horse his head for a bit and return to pick her up again, and they were doing these pleasant things together, maybe going somewhere where they could dismount and share treasured moments—— But it was not; that was Jean-Marc Roland disappearing into the distance through the trees, and he was a decidedly unknown quantity. Last night she had discovered that, for when he had decided to play kissing games with her she had, suddenly and quite spontaneously, done her share of the kissing. She had been seeking a part of the Jim she seemed to have lost, but it was not Jim in those depths she was plumbing but an entirely alien entity and, because it was not unattractive, dangerous.

The thunder of Fullani's hooves was now coming towards them. Marc tugged on the reins and the beast stopped and reared, its teeth bared and its eyes wild. Debbie thought, the man, his dog and his horse all match, somehow: there's a threat in them all.

'All right?' he asked, when he had his horse under complete control again and made him match Klara's trot.

'Yes, thanks. Fine. These horses aren't as big as ours in England, are they?'

'No. They're pure Arabs from the north. Fullani was given me by a Fullani chief, hence his name. They're bred to move, naturally, and to stand the climate. Hear that?'

Debbie listened and of course she could hear something. It was the lowing of cattle.

'My prize herd,' Marc said, and they trotted out of the trees on to a grassy plain, well fenced round a large herd of cattle. 'All attested,' he explained, as a boy wearing a cowboy sort of hat, but with the usual big grin, admitted them to the paddock by opening a gate.

'What's different about them from the hump-backed cattle we saw in small herds on the way here?' Debbie asked, glad she was seeing them from the comparative safety of a horse's back. Debbie had forgotten her country ways and was a bit nervous of cows. They had humps, like camels, and great curved horns. She kept close to Marc.

'The difference is that these are the progeny of Brahma cows and Charollais bulls. Like the horses they can stand the climate, but we're putting more meat on them by improving the stock. Can you bear to see my bulls without succumbing to sentiment and thinking

"Oh, poor things! Just kept there in sheds, fed fat and watered and only used for one very elementary purpose"?'

Feeling she was being tested in some way, Debbie said, 'I think I can bear it.'

The bulls were huge; fat, white, heavy and with a breadth of forehead that made them appear extremely fierce. They had rings through their noses and a chain tethering them. Two boys were mucking out and a third was obviously in charge. Marc had a few words with him. One of the bulls bellowed and Debbie jumped in her saddle and let the reins go. All in a moment Klara, who was obviously nervous of bulls, had broken into a gallop and dashed away. Debbie tried hanging on to the mare's mane but lost a stirrup. She began to slip from the saddle and yelled out in desperation and then she hit the ground with a thud, had all the wind knocked out of her, literally bit the dust and lay still.

Marc picked her up much as he had hauled her from the ditch, and stood her up against a tree while he felt her down for broken bones. She took her breath in in deep, painful gasps and choked on something. Two of the cattle-herders came running up and one was dispatched to recover the mare, which was now quietly grazing a hundred yards or so away.

'Are you all right?' Marc asked, wiping her face down with his handkerchief.

'I—I think so.'

'Right. Get aboard again and wallop her.'

'I—I don't think I can.'

'*Do as you're told.*' She felt rather as she had when ordered to get in the back of the Land-Rover, a kind of exhilaration of fear.

'Wallop her with the reins. Show her she can't do that sort of thing to you. If she takes off again then wallop her some more. Master the damned beast!'

Debbie lashed out blindly at Klara, though it

crippled her simply to sit astride the animal again, and tried to hang on with her sore knees as the creature broke from a trot into a gallop. She tugged on the reins, encouraged by Jean-Marc who rode alongside her, and brought the ends sharply down on the foam-flecked withers. As the bridle jarred uncomfortably the mare finally slowed into a walk, hanging her head.

'Now pat her, say she's a good girl,' encouraged Jean-Marc, 'but keep a hold on her. Let her know who's boss.'

Back in the compound of the bungalow Debbie rather thankfully watched the horses being taken off. Now she could limp in peace and count her innumerable bruises.

'Have a hot bath,' Marc recommended. 'There's just time before lunch. You came quite a cropper. Good girl for doing as you were told and getting back up again. It must have been quite an effort.'

'And we *had* to know who was boss, hadn't we?' Debbie asked, apparently innocently. But Marc gave her a very odd look as she limped off in the direction of his bathroom and then smiled appreciatively as he lit his pre-lunch pipe.

'How about a nice cold beer?' he asked her as she returned, once more in borrowed clothes, though this time a pair of his shorts was tied up with an old tie so that she was saved the indignity of hanging on to them.

'It sounds heavenly,' said Debbie, who normally hated the taste of beer. 'And the bath was heavenly, too. Actual running water! I could have wallowed and wallowed.'

'We have our own storage tanks. But so has the hospital. You mean you have no running water in your house?'

'No. I have a sort of watering-can arrangement of a shower, which has to be refilled every time I use it.'

'Oh, lord! I had one of those when I first came out.

Why are you so primitive?'

'Well, apparently a physiotherapist is an unknown quantity and whoever runs the hospital has allowed me a small hut without real facilities until I either prove my usefulness or am considered merely a liability. I only have a six-month contract. I'm supposed to have my main meals with Jim and Sister, and I suppose I could use Sister's bathroom, but I do rather value my independence and privacy. Now that I've got a steward to look after me I may spend quite a bit of my free time in my little house.'

'While you were bathing I was thinking about you and Jim. He's been out here just over a year, you say? He could be suffering from emotional lethargy without realising it. This country—this continent—affects Europeans in odd ways. The worst that can happen is that one can surrender one's entire initiative, drift along with the tide and become almost literally a piece of human flotsam, perhaps washed up and lying somewhere just to rot. A little of the worst has to be experienced to bring out the best in us. I came out with such plans, such ideas, and came up against such difficulties that I began to accept them and submit to them rather than attempt to surmount them.

'Lethargy is the curse of Africa,' he explained. 'You'll find mighty roads, beautifully built, suddenly running out in the middle of nowhere; the engineers will have been recalled to discuss some other project which has been considered necessary and must at least be started to please the pundits. That, too, may never actually be finished.

'But I must speak of myself, not of generalities. After about six months I found myself able to stare at a blank wall for two hours on end without actually feeling bored; my entertainment was to watch a lizard hunting flies or ants about their eternal activities. All the books I had brought, intending to read, lay still packed away and even reading my father's letters became an effort.

After a while I didn't answer them for months, though my intention was to do it next day. Always next day, *mañana*, the day which never comes. I wrote to Pascale, but my feelings for her were hidden by a mental blockage. I loved her, of course, but what was love? It was an active thing and I had become a passive creature, whose eight-hour day had been cut to six and then four hours and sometimes days when I didn't work at all. I grew a beard; who wanted to shave twice a day when one had discovered the bliss of the very core of idleness?

'It was Mary who dug me out of the pit. She came and berated me, made me shave and read me the riot act. We—the Europeans—had come out here to beat 'em, not to join 'em, she said. The inertia which had gripped me was something which killed in a much subtler way than the malaria of old had done. It was a kind of pernicious anaemia of the mind. The antidote was to work and to feed the mind—force-feed if necessary—and literally force one's will upon one's own self. I made myself work, and my boys, too, for they, too, had drifted into idleness, and I made myself unpack my books and read. I began to remember my feelings for Pascale, and long for her. To have her out there, with me, became my dominant ambition, but it may have been that my apathy had been conveyed to her in my letters, and so she had already begun to forget me. Apparently this sickness—for a kind of sickness it is—is fairly widespread and not at all unique. Your Jim, who will have had to do his stint of work under an African director, may have turned himself off in other ways. Did you notice anything by his letters?'

'Yes. Lately they've been reports of his various activities. He has described clinics he's held in minute detail. But he hasn't been very affectionate——'

'Ah! I think we may have hit the nail on the head. Your Jim has learned to live quite happily without emotional stimulation, as I learned to live without shaving. His entire life has become his doctoring, and then you arrive, with claims upon him of a different nature, which he can't actually remember. He can't replenish those wells of desire which have temporarily drained dry. It seems to me we have to provide a stimulus to alleviate the situation. Your releasing him from the engagement may have seemed a bit coquettish, but it does leave the field open for intruders.'

'Intruders?' Debbie echoed.

'Indeed, yes. I could be considered an intruder, couldn't I? I mean with my reputation and everything? If I began paying you attentions then Jim might wake up and threaten me with a horsewhip or something? I should quite enjoy that, and you could well enjoy the rising of the phoenix of your love life.'

'I don't think I ever heard such an audacious suggestion in all my life!' Debbie exclaimed, aghast. 'You know that we can't be together for more than an hour without me stepping on your corns. I love Jim, I know I do, deep down, and he loves me. But you, you—you——!'

'Yes, I know,' Marc smiled. 'But I only want to help. Think about it, anyway. If you need me you can invite me to dinner with your Jim and Sister Meadows. It's ages since I was at the hospital because I find them so boring—oh, I know your Jim must be wonderful, but I'm not in love with him—and I can meet Oduloru and Saba at the Club. Now I must take you home to have a siesta. You look very pretty when your eyes flash like that, and now that I really look at them they *are* brown.'

'Oh, you're impossible,' Debbie snapped. 'Will my clothes be ready? I can hardly go back looking like this.'

CHAPTER SIX

DEBBIE sat in Sister Meadows' rather pretty bungalow and sipped tea out of a floral china cup. Jim sat opposite her, occasionally glancing at her and smiling in a considering way, as though she was one of his patients whose diagnosis he had not quite succeeded in establishing.

'So you both had a nice time, eh?' she asked, with a reassuring answering smile in Jim's direction.

'Yes, indeed,' Sister answered. 'It's worth the journey just to have a change of air once in a while. Does one a power of good. Here we breathe steam. I mean, there it is, no arguing the fact. But here we are and it's here where we're needed. I would have insisted on your joining us, but it's important that you become acclimatised by meeting the actual conditions in which you'll be working. Two days nearer to tackling your job. Let me fill your cup.'

'Thanks. I must say you have everything very nice here, Sister.'

'It suits me. I had the china shipped out and, fortunately, only one saucer was broken when it arrived. I can't abide tea out of earthenware, and that's all you can get here. I made the curtains myself, and the cushion covers, too.'

'It's quite home from home. *And* an electric fan!' The fan stirred the hot air into a hot wind, but even that was mildly refreshing. 'I don't seem to have electricity in my house.'

'No, well don't worry too much about that. The generator is shut down at eight o'clock each evening, so we all have paraffin lamps and fridges. In any case electric things keep blowing up or breaking down and there aren't many electricians locally. Somebody will come pretending to know and promptly give himself an electric shock. Jim is quite a handyman.' She smiled across at him. 'I send for him, now, to do my odd jobs.'

'And what have you been doing with yourself, Debbie, while we've been gone?' Jim asked encouragingly. 'Sleeping the whole time, I shouldn't wonder!'

'Not at all,' Debbie said promptly. 'I've been very much occupied one way and another. First I got myself a steward-boy, then the Director came to see me with his smaller children—lovely little girls—and he took me into Okusha where he left me with his Land-Rover and chauffeur to do some shopping with Kadiri. I hadn't any cups, saucers or anything, so I had to make do with earthenware——' she smiled at Sister—'but it's prettily patterned and made in Stoke-on-Trent, so I don't suppose it's so bad. I bought food, and Kadiri—that's my steward—bought wood and nails and things and now I have shelves and am much more organised. The Director lent me some money and some things I had to charge to the hospital. It was all very enjoyable.'

'Good for you!' said Jim, and Sister also smiled her approval. 'But what do you mean when you say you got yourself a steward-boy? You mean Dr Oduloru brought him.'

'No. He was as surprised as I was. I mean, there I was the night before, not knowing if I would get a shower or not or a cup of tea, and next morning he was there, tea by my bed, windows open, the sheets washed and the mattress and pillows airing all before I could say Jack Robinson. Actually it was Kadiri who found me. The Director says he should be O.K., he looked at his pass-book——' she decided to say nothing about the Indian's accusing letter—'and he made Joshua lend him some decent clothes. Of course he's a Moslem, but I don't suppose that matters so long as he does his work. I've almost fallen over him twice today, prostrated towards Mecca. I——'

'Only Christian boys are employed by the hospital,' Sister Meadows said quietly. 'I think it might be a dangerous precedent, Miss Wyndham.'

'I don't see why. After all, I pay him out of my own salary, don't I?'

'It's not a question of payment, but of upsetting the other stewards. We are a Christian community, most of the boys we employ here have been educated at a mission school and understand our ways. Imagine if the operating-room steward was a Moslem and prostrated himself towards Mecca in the middle of an operation! Our boys have been severely vetted and passed every required test both of domesticity and honesty. I think allowing yourself to be taken over by this fellow was a grave blunder. You could be robbed or—or worse. I should get rid of him without further ado and I'll get Dawa to recommend someone in his place.'

'No, thank you,' Debbie said quite sharply, so that Jim looked at her in consternation. 'Joshua attacked Kadiri and there was a fight, but Dr Oduloru intervened and said it was no good calling oneself Christian and behaving like a heathen. I'm prepared to accept his ruling and give Kadiri a chance. As the Director said, we don't want to start a religious war.'

'Very well.' Eve Meadows looked up at Dawa with her ready smile and indicated that he could remove the tea-things. 'Who am I to override the hospital Director? So you got yourself a steward and went shopping. What then?'

'Then Kadiri wanted to give the house a good clean, so I took a walk.'

'I hope you keep your valuables locked up? Where's your engagement ring?'

Debbie looked at Jim, who lowered his eyes, so he obviously hadn't confided in Sister over the weekend.

'Oh, that's in safe keeping, and I haven't a lot of valuables. I'm sure Kadiri will guard what I possess.'

Jim said quickly, sensing animosity in Debbie towards Sister's probing, 'Where did you walk to?'

'Towards Kadiri's village and then down the road to Marc Roland's place. I decided on the spur of the moment to thank him for all his trouble.'

'That was too far to walk so early on,' Jim scolded. 'I left you behind believing you were going to rest up.'

'Well, I didn't think it was far, and anyway, *he* told me off about it, warned me about heat-stroke and so on. My head was thudding a bit, but he made me rest up and we had tea and so forth. I even stayed to dinner and then he ran me back. This morning he sent a car for me and we went riding out to see his herds, so you see I haven't had a dull moment.'

Sister rose and said, 'Perhaps, Jim, you'd like to take your fiancée over to your house to complete your chat? I must discuss dinner with Dawa and see to one or two things. Also I must pop over to the hospital and see how Janet's coped while I've been gone.'

Debbie said as she strolled by Jim's side across the compound, 'Were we ever so nicely dismissed from the presence? Have I disgraced myself yet again?'

Jim pondered as though trying not to answer too hastily. He then said, 'You were determined to see that chap at the first opportunity, weren't you? I've tried to warn you about him. If you'd wanted to thank him for services rendered you could have sent him a note. Your new steward-boy, who again you're being rather bloody-minded about, could have delivered it.'

Debbie went ahead of him into his bungalow. She seemed to see it as for the first time, as last night she had been too emotional, frightened and upset to really notice things. It was similar to Sister's in size but starkly masculine. There were no frills or flounces and the plain dark brown curtains were intended to keep out the light when necessary or shut out the gaze of intruders at night. They were not pretty. The china standing on a kind of sideboard was plain blue with white rims. Debbie wondered if Sister brought her own cup over when she came for a cup of tea or made do with this coarser earthenware. She felt a sort of lump in her throat which threatened tears if she tried to speak while it was still there, and she did not want her relationship with Jim to be used on womanly tears which would induce masculine comfort.

Eventually she felt herself to be in control again and ventured, 'No, I wasn't determined to see Marc Roland at the first opportunity, Jim. It was purely a spontaneous gesture on my part as I seemed to be headed in his direction. He could have been out; that was a chance I took. But I was glad to see him because my head was thudding a bit and I don't think I could have faced the walk home again just then. I know going out by myself, so soon, was a mistake, but who can say he never made one of those? But I won't hold anything against him on the say-so of others about his supposed reputation with women. It takes two, you know, and I suppose a good-looking single man is fair game. I'll bet if you'd gone about more they'd have been after *you*, and the reason I know you haven't mixed much with the community here is that Mary Tate told me, not Marc Roland. She said everybody wondered why you and Sister Meadows never went to the Club.'

Jim looked down at the rush mat. 'I didn't come out here for the life of a club, Debbie. I came out to work and to learn. I do my job and then I have my books.'

'Mary also said that all work and no play——'

'Damn Mary!' Jim said fiercely, looking up. 'Who is she, anyway? Some flibbertigibbet who has nothing to do but idle her time away at the wretched Club?'

Debbie had started at his show of vehemence. She thought, 'Oh, God, I don't even recognise Jim like this. I wanted us to get to know each other again and instead he's growing more into a stranger every minute.'

She said aloud, 'No, Mary is not in the least a flib-bertigibbet. She is African born of English parents who were teaching in Ibadan before the University came into being. She, too, is a teacher at the local High School. She's a Cambridge graduate and has a Ph.D. in African studies. I believe she's as dedicated to education as you are to your job, and she still counts Marc Roland among her friends, so he can't be such a bad lot. Also she attends the Club, as do the Director and Dr Saba.'

'So I'll take you to the Club some time,' Jim said, as though giving in to a persistent child for the sake of peace. He gave a long sigh.

Supper, at Sister's, was somehow a sober affair, and Debbie felt that Sister had been told the news of the broken engagement. Nobody seemed to have much appetite and Dawa had not exactly surpassed himself on this occasion, so that plates were removed which had merely been pecked at. The dessert was pancakes, rather leathery but edible, at least, and then a message came via one of the hospital stewards for Jim to go and look at a new admission in the hospital.

'Send word if you need me,' said Sister, and began to pour coffee for Debbie and herself after dismissing Dawa for the night.

'How could you do it to him?' she asked at length. 'How could you?'

Debbie decided to be obtuse.

'How could I do what?' she asked.

'Well, breaking your engagement at a time like this?'

'A time like what?' Debbie asked again.

'Just when he has to study so hard for his Master's certificate? He was planning to go home next year, take his exam and probably get married and then come out here again, with you, to apply for a senior job, maybe as a lecturer at the Medical School in Ibadan. He's devoted to Nigeria and I would count it an honour and a privilege to be married to a man like that.'

All this was said without anger, which Debbie found irritating, but rather in a tone of gentle reproof. She thought it would humanise Sister Meadows to throw a tantrum occasionally, and actually look ruffled.

'Well, I'm sorry, Sister, naturally, but I think Jim understands better than you do why we couldn't just go ahead with any prearranged plans. Plans are made with one's head, but human hearts have a habit of coming to their own conclusions. I don't think I would be a helpmeet to Jim at the moment if I kept him tied to me. Please understand that I'm interested in his career, too. It's better for him to be free until he's taken his Master's certificate.'

Sister cleared her throat and said in the chummiest of voices, 'You don't think you've had your head turned a little by that—that charmer of a Roland, do you? Because he can be—very charming.'

'On the whole he hasn't been charming to me,' Debbie all but snapped. 'Nobody has anything to do with the way Jim and I feel—or rather, don't feel—at present. I wish we could let the subject drop.'

'Well, if you appear to be openly taking up with someone the moment you've rejected your fiancé, you must expect other people to put two and two together. You've remarked on the way the human heart behaves, and the observer, who sees things with his head, may be nearer the mark than you imagine.'

'Please do shut up!' Debbie said sharply.

Sister lowered long dark lashes over those strange pale eyes of hers but otherwise showed no emotion. Debbie rose and walked round the room. She picked up a silver cigarette box and examined the engraved figures without really seeing them.

'It belonged to my father,' Sister said as she replaced it on the small table.

'Oh. You mean the box?'

'Yes. He was a heavy smoker and he died of lung cancer. Both lungs were affected so operation was pointless. It hasn't contained any cigarettes since, I can tell you.'

'I'm sorry about your father. It must have been horrible, you being a nurse and knowing what was going to happen in the end.'

'No. I was the last to know, as a matter of fact. My home was in Alnwick—that's in Northumberland—and I rarely got home. Mother wouldn't allow me to be told. She thought it might affect my work, which of course it would have, and it wasn't as though I could do anything. It was all over when I knew, and Mother was very brave and independent. She wouldn't have me leave Matthew's, where I was due for promotion, and so my memories of Father were as he was, strong and handsome, and always searching for a cigarette from that box.' She grimaced prettily. 'For me it was as though his illness never was. I wasn't involved. It almost left me—untouched. That's what our job does for one, it takes the sting out of death and alienates one, subtly, from one's family. The family that really matters is the one in the ward at that time.'

Debbie thought that either Sister Meadows successfully kept her emotions hidden or was incapable of deep feeling. Her own father's death had desolated her, and she, too, had had her own job to do at the time, but had done it as a means of assuaging her grief rather than allowing it to engulf her. But grief had been real and she had cried herself to sleep at nights, had cried in her mother's arms and been fiercely glad when both Mother and Jill had joined in. Dr Wyndham had been truly mourned by his family in the way that Debbie was sure nature intended, and now she looked at Sister Meadows with her marble-smooth brow and calm, clear eyes and wondered if she was one of those oddities destined never to climb the emotional heights or plumb their depths. Debbie could still not have spoken of her father's death in such detail without remembering how it had felt at the time and being affected by it.

She was glad that Jim returned at that moment as she had nothing more to say to Sister. She announced that she was going to bed and he automatically held out her cardigan and said he would see her to her house.

'I hear you're hoping to take your M.S. next year?' she asked, as a horned insect flew into her face with quite a bump.

'Yes. Sister told you, did she?'

'That's so. She seemed to think I may have put you off, harmed your chances in some way.'

Jim actually laughed. 'What rubbish! Nothing will put me off where I'm set to go careerwise.'

'I thought not. Well, goodnight, Jim.'

'Goodnight.' They didn't kiss, but Debbie would have been glad for Jim to make the gesture if he felt so inclined. She would certainly have played her part in the exchange. In a way she felt as though she was once more in mourning. Every moment she spent in Jim's company put yet another nail in the coffin of their romance. It was sad enough to make her want to cry, but she never actually got around to it.

CHAPTER SEVEN

ROUNDS at Okusha hospital were much the same as at any English hospital, apart from the fact that the patients were black and stubble-haired, men and women alike, though a woman, when she was feeling better, would attempt to braid her hair in hundreds of tiny plaits, or a friend she had made on the ward would do it for her. They spent hours doing one another's hair, and it was a kind of therapy, for, of course,

Okusha hospital did not run to such luxuries as occupational therapists. Dr Oduloru led main rounds on Mondays and Thursdays, with a complete retinue following him of which Debbie now trailed at the rear. She had been working for over a week and though, for a day or two, she had felt the heat sufficiently to feel like fainting on occasions, she was now becoming used to it, though she looked forward to the afternoon break when all and sundry of the staff were released for two hours' siesta, apart from one nurse who was left in charge, and, as most of the patients would be sleeping, probably nodded off herself at times.

Jim did a round every other day of the week, apart from weekends, though he was usually only accompanied by Sister on these occasions. Dr Saba's rounds, as the senior physician, were not taken very seriously, but Dr Iloro would report anything he thought needed reporting to Debbie, if he thought a medical patient would benefit from physiotherapy. A bronchial patient was thus brought to her notice who needed breathing exercises to help clear his bronchial tubes, and a child who had lain a long time suffering from a fever, which was noted for relapsing periodically, and had grown very weak, had her wasted limbs massaged and exercised in bed so that when she was eventually declared to be over the fever she could walk on wobbly legs up and down the ward.

On this day Debbie's mind was wandering, which normally would have been inexcusable, but she was secretly worried. It was hot, as usual, and the fans busy in the ward merely stirred the hot air and ruffled the pages of notes in their folders or the book one was trying to write in, and they stirred the hair on the top of one's head, which was dry, and discovered the wet hair underneath, a most uncomfortable feeling. Debbie envied Sister, who looked so immaculate always in her pretty cap. She herself felt like a golliwog and tried to dodge the nearest draught. Flies buzzed in all the windows. As all the doors and shutters were open, except those which kept out the probing fingers of the sun, there was always this constant buzzing of flies. Sometimes they even descended when a wound was being dressed and the nurse would quickly look to make sure Sister wasn't looking and then cover up the sore smartly. Flies, ants and mosquitoes were the curse of this continent, Debbie was finding. One could never beat them and had to be content with controlling the pests as best one could.

'Miss Wyndham, would you join us, please?' came the basso profundo of Dr Oduloru's voice into her thoughts on this occasion, and she jumped, finding the other members of the procession smiling and frowning at her equally. Dr Saba smiled and so, gently, did Dr Iloro, who liked her, because she took care to be kind and deferential to him as his status demanded. Sister looked questioning and slightly grieved, as she always worked by the clock and the round was taking longer than it should. Jim frowned and breathed out loudly through his nose. The staff nurse frowned, too, to please him.

'I'm sorry, sir,' she said contritely. 'You were saying——?'

'This chap here has a very weak and wasted thigh. Can you do anything about it, do you think? I can't operate on the knee until his muscles will support the leg.'

Debbie moved up and felt the large thigh muscle. The staff nurse held the leg and bent the knee, ignoring the patient's groans as Debbie still felt and probed.

'What's the trouble, sir?' she asked.

'He has a splinter in the joint and it may have been in for years. He's been walking stiff-legged. When I remove the splinter I obviously don't want to leave him with a stiff leg, but it's better if, until I operate, the joint is immobilised. Well?'

'I'll try to build up the muscle in a fortnight, sir.

Will that be all right?'

'Do your best, Miss Wyndham. Normally we can't afford to keep our beds occupied so long, but if we let him go he'll carry his stiff leg to the grave.'

Debbie wrote the man's name in her book, and the number of his bed. She would be back after rounds to start working on him. She gave him a small, promissory smile and followed the procession.

It was worrying how Kadiri was behaving suddenly. She daren't confide in either Sister or Jim, who would say they had told her so. Suddenly Kadiri had become light-fingered, not by robbing her but other people for her. She remembered the morning she had seen the silver cigarette box shining in the morning light on the small window table in her living-cum-dining-room. There was a vase always kept on it which Kadiri filled with flowers from the bush. He thought this custom of Europeans rather quaint and had laughed the first time she had brought home a bunch of flowers and put them in water. As he told her, flowers were for outside, in bush, and inside was for peoples. But he regularly changed the flowers, for they did not last long in that heat, and one day she found a large yellow flower in the vase, with a crimson tongue, which she was convinced was some kind of orchid. But the silver box could only belong to one person, and that was Sister. Debbie had asked Kadiri where it had come from. At times her English was beyond him and she had to bring it down to his level. She finished up with, 'Where you get this?'

'I no get,' he smiled. 'You get. I clean him. Now shine good.'

'But, Kadiri, it's not mine. It's Sister's.'

'Not yours? Of course it yours. It in your house. You no like?'

'Of course I like. But I'm taking it back.'

Fortunately Sister was in her bathroom and her sitting-room stood empty. Debbie replaced the box feeling extremely guilty. She hoped it had not been missed.

A couple of days later a carved ivory musical box appeared on her table. Kadiri lifted the lid and let it play "The Campbells are Coming". He seemed delighted with it. 'You like better than other one?' he asked.

'And where you get that?' she asked with a sharp frown.

He started back as though stung by her tone. 'I not play music again,' he said. 'I sorry. I think you like.'

'Kadiri,' she said seriously, 'you are to stop taking things from other people. Do you understand? Now take the musical box back to wherever you got it from.'

He picked up the box and disappeared without a word, but later in the day she had discovered it in the kitchen on top of the small fridge. She had enquired among the hospital servants as to who owned a musical box and had discovered it was the Director's property. Returning it to his bungalow she had encountered Joshua, who looked with dawning intelligence at the article.

'So Missie had the box all the time? I couldn't find. I tell Director. He say I no proper look.'

Debbie had not enlarged on the subject but had discovered herself eating with strange cutlery next morning. The knives, forks and spoons she had bought for herself in Okusha town were of a distinctly utilitarian variety, but the spoon with which she ate her cereal was solid silver and richly engraved. The butter knife was the same. She rushed into the kitchen where Kadiri was singing quietly, brandishing the two implements.

'Where——?' she asked.

'Very nice, eh, missie?' Kadiri showed her the rest of the 'loot'—knives, forks and spoons all to match. He then picked up one of her own forks and bent it in two. 'These very bad,' he told her. 'I take to shop get money back.'

'Kadiri,' she said, white-faced, 'I want you to go home. Just go.'

'Not day off,' he complained, with a puzzled frown. 'Not Friday. I got work to do.'

'No, you haven't!' she shouted. 'Go home at once! Go on!'

In spite of what he was apparently doing he had a dignity which he now donned like a cloak, and without a word he turned and walked away. A few minutes later she found his green pyjama suit neatly folded and he was disappearing into the trees in his ragged singlet and shorts.

'Come back in the morning!' she called, not knowing why she should feel so mean when she was so sadly being proved wrong in her judgment.

That was why her thoughts wandered on this morning during rounds, and when they retired to Sister's office for coffee she jumped when Dr Saba said blithely, 'We seem to have had ruddy burglars in the night, isn't it? Haven't had time to check what's missing altogether, but that night-watch ought to be shot.'

Sister said quietly, 'I don't think you should delay taking old Granny Kobo off her drip, Doctor. She has so many bed-sores that she needs to be put on her tummy, and as she seems determined to die—well, we'll just have to let her die in peace. The Director did say do it immediately.'

'Oh, well!' Dr Saba said cheerfully. 'That was a nice sip of coffee while it lasted. I am going now, this very minute.'

'I'll come and help turn the poor old thing,' Debbie said, putting down her own half-finished coffee.

Granny Kobo was the old woman who imagined somebody had put a ju-ju on her and was now merely being kept alive by a drip. Her body had wasted, how-ever, and her kidneys failed. She was covered in sores which were becoming septic and it had been decided to allow her the dignity of natural death. Debbie wondered what would be put on the death certificate: was ju-ju considered a valid cause of death? Apparently when the old woman had been admitted her legs were paralysed, but she was otherwise quite fit and had merely submitted to what she imagined was a curse put upon her. Dr Oduloru, who knew that many of his countryfolk were still riddled with superstition, accepted the fact that all had been done for her that could be done and that where death had taken place in the spirit it was only kind to let the body follow.

'Dr Saba,' she asked the young physician, as he rather clumsily removed the drip-needle, not thinking the old woman could feel anything, 'have you lost any silver?'

'Now how could you be knowing that, dear Miss Wyndham, when Sister so abruptly shut me up just now?'

'Because I've found some silver—er—near my house. Engraved with human figures.'

'Of course, a family heirloom from my great-great-granddaddy's day, and with scenes taken from the Khama Sutra, no less. Not that you would know anything about that, my dear young lady, but we Indians have never been known for repressing or denying the beauty of primitive human urges.'

'Well, I can return your silver,' Debbie said quickly. 'I'll do so when we break this afternoon.'

'You would not like a game of tennis, then, would you? I find I do not need siesta. After all, I am suited to the climate. Just pleasantly tanned, I think?' he fingered his pale coffee skin with a self-loving smile.

'I'm not up to tennis in the afternoon yet, Doctor,' Debbie apologised, glad to have discovered the owner of the silver. 'Please don't be hard on the night-watch. If you make a fuss you may have everybody getting scared to sleep at night.'

With the aid of the senior nurse on duty they turned the old woman over, whipping the pillows away. The nurse went for her dressing trolley as other untreated sores were exposed. Very gently, but firmly, Debbie took the old woman's head and turned it to one side. There was a distinct click, and a sharp gasp came from the patient, whose emaciated limbs immediately began to twitch. Debbie looked up at an equally surprised Dr Saba. 'She's not unconscious, you know,' she told him. 'She's looking at me. I thought for one moment I'd broken her neck.'

'Or else you've dislodged whatever was paralysing her in the first place,' said the doctor excitedly. 'Send somebody for Iloro. He's learnt their lingo and can maybe get through to her, isn't it?'

Dr Iloro came and stuck needles in parts of the old body. There were gratifying reactions, one of which was unbearable pain, but that was countered by morphia. Before the old woman slipped into sleep she had managed to converse with Dr Iloro.

'She said she looked into a white face, and it told her the ju-ju was lifted,' he said with a broad smile. 'She said now she'll get better and see her grandchildren again. Well done!' he told Debbie.

'I don't know anything about ju-ju,' she denied, 'but if she thinks that then I'll certainly help her to get better. I do know something about physiotherapy, and she's going to need plenty of that.'

During the break for siesta she lay sleeplessly on her bed, having returned Dr Saba's silver to the bungalow he shared with Iloro, and thought about the old woman who might now very likely live to return to her village, if her will to live was as strong as her submission to the imagined ju-ju had been, and also about what she was to do with Kadiri. She wondered if the time had come to confide in Jim, asking him to help her with the problem and guide her in the future, but having made up her mind not to use her past relationship with

Jim to influence him on her behalf, she also wondered if it might not be better to take the Director into her confidence. Both Jim and Sister rather put Dr Oduloru at the tip of the peak of administration, and implied that he was not to be approached directly by lesser members of the staff, but only through either of them in the first instance. Debbie, however, had always found him most approachable since that first day when she had visited him in his office. He had brought his children to see her and offered her the use of his transport and had seen to it that life in her little hut was at least made tolerable. She fancied discussing Kadiri with him in preference to Jim, and determined to do it that very evening. She had told Jim and Sister that she had no intention of dining in a threesome every night.

'You had a very amicable arrangement before I came,' she had said last night, 'and I simply feel I'm intruding. After all, I am only an experiment, in a way, and after my six months may be sent packing. I can dine in my own place, and sometimes you can visit me, one at a time. Kadiri's quite a good cook, so he says, and he minds when I go out every night.'

She considered the 'gifts' Kadiri had acquired for her. First there had been Sister's silver cigarette box, secondly the Director's musical box and thirdly Dr Saba's erotically-carved but nevertheless valuable cutlery. If the steward was doing a round of all the bungalows then Jim's was obviously the next in line. She wondered what Jim possessed that Kadiri might fancy for her, and decided it could well be the silver and crystal rose-bowl which had been his going-away present from his friends and colleagues at St Matthew's. She decided to give Kadiri just one more chance before going to see the Director about him. If Jim's rose-bowl turned up in her house then she would take both him, and it, straight to Dr Oduloru. She suspected that Kadiri's English wasn't up to much. He would have to be told in his own language exactly what he had done to offend and then accept his dismissal.

Realising she was not going to be able to sleep she got up again, being without a steward again, made herself a cup of tea. She would miss Kadiri, for he seemed to anticipate her needs and requirements beautifully. He would somehow have known she was sleepless and have appeared with the cup that cheers by now. She daren't shower because there was no one to clear up after her and refill the tank, but she compromised by dabbing herself all over with a damp flannel and then donned her uniform for the second spell of duty.

Old Granny Kobo was holding her own and had taken a little nourishment from a feeding cup. Sister approached Debbie.

'Well, it seems we've witnessed a small miracle,' she smiled, in her usual calm and unruffled way, though her eyes were at the same time scanning the ward to make sure everybody who should be was working.

'Yes. Isn't it wonderful?' Debbie asked.

'It is. Of course the real miracle was the drip-feed which kept our old Granny alive long enough for the imagined ju-ju to wear its way out. There never was anything wrong with the old thing. It was all in the imagination. She's been examined over and over again and X-rayed. If she also imagines you personally had anything to do with her recovery I wouldn't play on it. I mean——' here a light laugh—'if it is imagined you have supernatural powers, you could be called out to deal with other cases concerned with ju-ju and not be able to do anything. You understand?'

'Yes, I do understand,' Debbie said levelly.

She worked through the long afternoon under a kind of strain. Not only were the heat and flies tiresome, but most of the patients didn't yet quite understand her function. Young men, particularly, seemed to find her ministrations amusing. They joked and obviously teased each other as she removed plasters and massaged and exercised ebony limbs. They became peculiarly limp when she was supposed to get them out of bed, so that she had to do more for them than she had imagined necessary.

Jim called her to him on one occasion and stood with her outside the ward. Her heart leapt as she imagined he was going to say something like, 'It's no good, Debbie, I can't stand it the way we are! We have to talk. Tonight at my place, or yours?' Instead he said, 'I'm picking up quite a bit of their lingo and the young chaps are taking the mickey out of you. They've probably never touched a woman and suddenly they find one who not only sees their bodies but works on them. They're enjoying it, in quite the wrong way. You do understand?' she was asked for the second time that afternoon.

'How could I fail?' she said, and her cheeks were pink with embarrassment. 'What am I supposed to do about it? They're on my list,' and she waved her book in front of him.

'Well, you must be like Sister and separate yourself from your job. Sister can do anything and she's not regarded as a sexual object. The young men don't giggle when she handles them. You mustn't flaunt yourself, Debbie.'

'Flaunt?' she echoed. 'Flaunt?' She looked down at her white overall with its green piping and asked again, 'What am I flaunting, for heaven's sake?'

'Well, isn't the neck of your blouse a little low? I mean, I'm taller than you and I can see——' he coughed and very slowly she turned up the revers of her overall and fastened them with a button hidden under the collar.

'Sorry,' she said. 'I didn't realise I was turning my patients on. I mean, when I failed to turn you on how could I know I still had the power?'

She half turned away when he said, 'Debbie, we'll have a trip to the Club soon. You need some fun. We all do.'

'Yes, of course,' she said, to put an end to that embarrassing exchange. She was glad when the day ended and the night staff took over, sorry when she arrived at her house to find no Kadiri there to greet her. As she had cut herself off from the tripartite dinner parties, she now had to find herself something to eat and had a most unsatisfactory meal of a couple of minute African eggs, one of which turned out to be coddled, and bread from which she had to cut lumps of mould. Everything in that climate went mouldy quickly. Normally Kadiri would have gone shopping in the late afternoon when the shops in Okusha town reopened and he always tested any eggs before cooking them. Any bad ones he would take back next day and make an exchange. How he did these things she didn't know, and she felt miserably inadequate trying to cope for herself. She missed being able to use the shower, too, but knew her need first thing in the morning, after the night's perspiration, was greater. Kadiri would be back in the morning anyway, and maybe he wouldn't steal anything else and all would be well again. She tried to read a book, but couldn't. She had real hunger pangs and took two bananas, blew out the lamp and, peeling the first banana, decided to go for a little walk.

She had got over her fear of the unknown. If she saw a pair of red animal eyes she would know it was only Wolf, the dog, and refuse to be intimidated by him. Kadiri had told her they all knew Master Roland's dog; even the 'pickins' were not afraid of him. Once, he had told her excitedly, the wolf dog had made puppies with a bitch in his village. There was a great demand for the offspring which all had some of the characteristics of their sire. Of course he had not told her this in these words, but in his own quaint pidgin English. Debbie had laughed as he had illustrated with his hands how some puppies had one pricked ear and one hanging down. She had seen the village dogs and the bitches always seemed to either have puppies or be heavily pregnant. There was no question, in these parts, of keeping a bitch in heat a prisoner. Here, nature was still in the raw in many ways, as she had now been advised to perceive in her young male patients. She determined to work hard on her male trainee, Oliver, and then turn him loose on the men. Tundi Agele, her female trainee, a rather superior type of girl, refused to enter the men's ward, and now Debbie knew why. Tundi had expressed a wish to be taught to help handicapped children, and there were plenty of those about.

Debbie stilled her hunger pangs with the second banana and looked about her. There was a certain magic in a tropical night. Scents pervaded the still air and mist writhed ghostlike among the trees. Over and above the sweet-scented things was the smell of decay and of festering vegetation. The bush fed on itself, enriching itself with things that died and lay rotting all about.

From the village came the usual chantings and the sound of drums. How did the babies manage to sleep? she wondered. But they did. They slept when they were tired and were bright-eyed and bonny, fastened in bright cloths to their mothers' backs, during the day. As the bitches all had puppies, so had the young women babies, or led a toddler by the hand during another pregnancy. Young girls over the age of puberty were somehow kept hidden. Debbie had never seen a girl when she walked through the village. Soon, she supposed, her friend Dina would disappear from view and emerge, in due course, a young wife and proudly pregnant. In these terms life seemed incredibly simple and preordained. One didn't have to find one's own mate or be troubled by the freedom of being allowed to fall in love, possibly with the wrong person. One was betrothed and, suddenly, there he was, the man with whom one would spend one's life and who would father one's children, and the seal that was set on the alliance was the approval of both sets of parents and the bride-price duly met. Did a girl stop to think that she was merely a viable proposition to her parents? No, she was content to live the life her tribe had lived for centuries, to carry on their traditions. It was all very well so long as the twentieth century was not allowed to intrude too much. In providing the fancy cooking pots it was accepted, as also were its tools and technical knowledge, but once it gave a girl ideas about her rights it was quickly stamped upon.

Debbie turned for home and stopped as she saw a nearby bush alive with fairy lights. Or, they were not exactly fairy lights but fireflies, swarming, and each tiny lantern was like a little bit of a star floated down from heaven. She then saw a faint light coming alongside the tennis court, which was quickly dowsed. It could only be Jim coming to see her, she decided, and her heart began to beat fit to burst. She would be ready for him. If his need for her had awakened in his heart then she would be most accommodating.

But no voice whispered 'Debbie!' and nobody knocked on her door. She saw the shadow of a white-clad figure—it was a moonless night—but it was to the back of the house that it went. She silently let herself into the sitting-room and waited, her finger on her torch at the ready, and heard the connecting door from the kitchen open with a slight creak. This time she would catch him red-handed, in the act. As soon as she felt another presence in the room she switched on the torch and lit up the tall figure of Dawa, still in his white steward's clothes with the brass buttons. In his hand he held not a rose-bowl but a tennis-racquet, which Debbie recognised as Jim's. She had given it to him the Christmas before he had come out here.

The steward had put up his hand against the light, but she said sternly, to let him know he had been recognised. 'So, Dawa, it was you bringing me presents, was it? Why did you do it? Why?'

The steward's shoulders drooped and he seemed to shrink before her eyes. He made to leave, but she said sharply, 'No, don't go. I want to hear your side of things or else I'll have to go straight to Sister and tell her what's been going on. Sit down. I won't eat you.' She lit the lamp and looked at him, but he could not meet her eyes.

'I so ashamed,' he moaned quietly, and actually seemed to be weeping. 'I so ashamed, missie.'

'Are you really ashamed, Dawa?' she asked, 'or is it just because you've been found out?'

He snivelled for a further few moments and then produced a grubby red and white handkerchief from the pocket of his pants and blew his nose. 'No, I ashamed for myself. I feel bad every time I do this. But I do it for all Christians, like myself,' and his eyes actually flashed at her.

'You can't make a bad thing good by calling yourself a Christian,' she told him. 'It was a bad thing to do, whoever had done it. Now you'd better tell me the whole story and why you did these bad things, or else we have to go to the doctor and report you.'

'No, no, please, missie!' he begged her. 'I tell why. My father work this hospital when missionary men make it. He was converted to Christian. Before that he leopardman, used to kill peoples, but he see error of ways.' Debbie knew Dawa must have learnt this phrase parrot-fashion and was probably proud of it. 'Always I go to church. All my brothers and sisters baptised proper, and only me have Nigerian name, Dawa, my father's and grandfather's name, means first-born.'

'I see,' Debbie said, becoming interested despite herself.

'I am confirmed. I know Creed. Sometimes I go confession. That why I feel bad about these things I do. I got to tell priest some day soon. But not too many Christians in Nigeria; many, many Mohammedans. This hospital always run by Christian boys, and your boy is not Christian.'

'Ah, so you've been trying to get Kadiri into disgrace, have you?'

'My brother Jonathan would have made very good steward-boy for Missie. I could have teached him. That boy, Kadiri, he come to our mission school for two year. We all fight him. He not one of us. He only come to school to learn English speaking.'

'But Kadiri is a very good steward-boy,' Debbie said, 'and even the Director said it was not Christian to judge him for his religious views. Do all the other stewards think like you?'

'Joseph, he mad he have to lend his clo's, but later he laugh about it. I not tell anybody what I do. I want everybody to think him thief.'

Debbie just looked at him and the dark eyes fell before her gaze.

'I nothin' better than a goddamned thief!' he said, crying again, 'and I so ashamed. What I do, missie? I feel so bad in heart,' and he put a hand to his chest.

'Well, I think you'd better see your priest about that, Dawa, but *I* won't say anything to anybody if you promise to stop trying to blacken Kadiri's character. You see, if Kadiri really did steal anything, I would think it was you. You do understand that? Now I think you'd better put that racquet back in Dr Brant's bungalow.'

'How you know it Dr Brant's?'

'Because I gave it to him,' Debbie said. 'We were——' she hesitated—'friends, and working at the same hospital. It cost me a lot of money. I recognised it immediately.'

'Then you forgive me, missie? You already sack Kadiri?'

'No, but I was very angry with him and he didn't seem to know why. If you hadn't spent so much time fighting with him at school he might have learnt better English. I sent him home after I found Dr Saba's silver. I've had nobody looking after me today.'

'I sorry. Something I can do for Missie?'

'No, thank you. He'll be back in the morning, I hope. If he doesn't come I shall expect you to go to his village and explain why I was angry.'

'Yes, missie. I go now.'

She sat pondering after Dawa's departure on the disruptive effect of her employment at the hospital so far. She had upset both Jim's and Sister's quiet and harmonious social life, given the young men patients in the hospital ideas and food for lewd jokes and now introduced a Moslem into a Christian community, thus causing Dawa's spiritual lapse from grace.

Well, at least she was glad Kadiri hadn't been light-fingered. That was a great load off her mind, but she couldn't help wondering how much Dawa's conscience would really have troubled him had the lad actually been dismissed from her service, probably without ever really knowing why.

Next morning she awoke and there was no tea by her bed, the shutters had not been opened. So he *had* been upset by her anger and decided to leave her. She couldn't blame him. She threw off the damp sheet and miserably contemplated getting up. Then there was the sound of hurrying feet and her room door opened quietly. Kadiri smiled almost shyly.

'Tea, missie? Make you feel better. You not so good yesterday, no? Got bellyache, maybe? Much bellyache in dis place.'

'Thank you, Kadiri.' She was so glad to see him she could have embraced him. 'I wasn't very good yesterday, but better today.' She took the tea gratefully as he tucked up the mosquito net and flung wide the shutters.

'I got treat for brekfus,' he told her. 'Get up. Have shower. Not be too long.'

As she was dressing, after her shower, she couldn't make out what Kadiri was cooking, but it smelled delicious and her gastric juices were working overtime. Normally she had a cereal beakfast, followed by a couple of the greenish oranges which were unpeelable but, when cut in half, proved to be eminently suckable. Cereals were inclined to become damp once they had been opened, but on this morning Debbie sat down at table in quite a fever of expectancy. Of course she was starving after not having had a proper supper last evening.

Kadiri entered with something on a large plate. He whipped off the lid and she exclaimed, 'Kippers!' Two fat kippers lay side by side on the plate and Kadiri had even put a knob of her supply of tinned butter on them. 'Wherever did you get kippers, Kadiri?'

The steward grinned as he put down a plate of bread and butter—he had brought a fresh loaf in with him—and then disappeared quickly for the coffee and marmalade. He began to pour before he spoke.

'This morning steward come from Master Roland's house. He say I be sure cook you for breakfus. He say you like.'

'Oh, I do!' Debbie agreed. It was a long time since she had tasted anything so delicious.

'He give me letter for you.' Kadiri felt in the pocket of his pyjama suit; he now had his own uniforms, which fitted his slight figure better than Joseph's borrowed plumes had done. He wore a pair of brown plastic sandals, though Debbie noticed he always left these at the entrance to the kitchen and went home barefoot. 'What Missie say call dis fishes?' he asked interestedly.

'Kippers. They're herrings, really.'

Kadiri tried to look intelligent without much success. 'I no get kipper or herrin' in Nigeria, but one day I cook Missie tiger-fish from river.'

'Tiger-fish?' Debbie asked.

'Yes. Got big teeth. Bite foot off.'

'Thank you very much,' said Debbie, shuddering as the lad disappeared kitchenwards.

She opened Marc Roland's letter with interest. His script was strange, almost gothic, and she remembered that he had been schooled in Switzerland during the years when one's writing is formed.

Dear Debbie,

    Having once spent a holiday in Scotland I became fond of kippers. A friend sends me a box out about four times a year and I hope you enjoy such things for breakfast, as I do. Have not heard your S.O.S., so presume all is well with you,

Sincere regards
Marc.

She wondered about the S.O.S. part of the message and remembered that he had offered his services in helping to restimulate Jim's interest in her. Funny how already a fortnight had fled since that conversation. Time was indeed a thief in this climate. Days passed uncounted and became weeks and in no time at all, if she didn't watch out, her six months would steal by and be unaccounted for.

She felt satisfied and much more contented after her meal and cleaned her teeth well after it. On the wards, however, Jim suddenly stopped and said, 'I can smell kippers, or am I dreaming?'

Debbie, who was tacking after him with Sister, said, 'That must be me. I've had kippers for breakfast. A present from the veterinary officer.' She realised that the smell must be coming from the letter which she was carrying in her pocket, which would have been pressed, by the courier, against the fishy parcel.

'I'll go and wash my hands again,' she said, 'though I did think I'd scrubbed the smell off.'

She tore up the note, with a kind of regret, and flushed it down the staff toilet, washed her hands and rejoined the procession.

During the coffee break Jim said, 'We're going to

the Club tonight, Debbie. Sister and I have decided
we're a couple of dull old things in the rest of the community's eyes. We'll have our meal up there. O.K.?'

'I hope you're not doing this just for me,' Debbie
said.

'No, we're not. Saba and Iloro are going, too. The
Director says he'll stand watch here. Saba's got a big
Mercedes and we're all piling into that. Half past eight
O.K. with you?'

'I'll be ready,' said Debbie.

CHAPTER EIGHT

AT the Club were parties of Africans and Indians scat-
tered about, Indians with other Indians and Africans
with Africans. They were the only truly international
group present, and maybe this was because their pro-
fession made them brothers, and sisters, under the
skin.

Saba had told them they were his guests on this occasion, as he was the only registered member of the
Club, but Jim said they would all join 'if it was any
good'.

'You have to be proposed and seconded, you know,'
Ranji said with a sly little smile, 'and one of your pro-
posers has to be a Nigerian.' His mirth suddenly
exploded. 'Can you imagine the British in India allowing any damn native into their club? Now the boot is
on the other foot, isn't it?'

Fortunately a waiter came for their order at that
moment, for Jim had grown very pink both with embarrassment and indignation.

They nearly all decided on the curry, which
Nigerians did very attractively with numerous side
dishes of peppers and tomatoes, coconut and orange

segments. Only Dr Saba risked ordering the mutton, for meat could be extremely tough from the stringy animals which reached the slaughterhouse. Fresh fruit salad followed the main course and they had drunk a couple of bottles of South African rosé, apart from Ranji, who never touched alcohol. They then went into the main lounge for coffee and were beset by other Club members, who came over to welcome them. Thus they met the Thompsons, a colonel and his lady, who had decided not to leave Nigeria upon his retirement from the Army. Their buff-complexioned daughter was with them, just recovering from a bout of malaria. She was so plain and unattractive that Debbie was surprised to hear she was married to a groundnut plantation manager. Of course, at that time she hadn't met the husband. Mary Tate came over and said, 'Well, I'm glad you hospital people have decided to let us out of Coventry. We really thought you didn't want to know us.'

'Sorry!' said Jim. 'Sister and I didn't realise we were appearing standoffish. I'm reading for my Master's certificate and Sister is nearly always on call—we're rather short-staffed in the upper echelons of nursing—but I'm sure we'd both have made the effort if we'd known what we were missing.'

Mary turned to Dr Iloro. 'Come with me and I'll introduce you to one or two people. You're from Uganda, aren't you?'

Debbie liked Mary very much for that gesture. Iloro was shy and still very unsure of himself and he had been quite amazed by the other's invitation in a 'fancy her noticing me!' way.

'Who would like to see the swimming pool?' Dr Saba asked. 'It's never used in the evening—everyone is too dressed up—but it is a very nice pool.'

'I'm enjoying my coffee,' Sister said, 'so I'll stay and finish it.'

'If you've seen one swimming pool, you've seen

them all,' said Jim.

'I'll come with you,' said Debbie, as she saw Ranji's countenance drop. 'I'm never tired of looking at swimming pools, and if I'm going to become a member here I'll need to know my way around.'

They walked round wide verandas, where people were enjoying drinks and chatting, with Ranji being greeted here and there and introducing Debbie to his particular cronies, and then they reached the pool, which gleamed blue and inviting and was lit underwater. The trees all around were hung with fairy lights. There were rows of changing cubicles at each end.

'It looks very inviting,' commented Debbie, who was perspiring profusely and yet knew there was a chill in the damp air. 'I'll be glad to make use of that one hot Saturday afternoon. That's if I get proposed and seconded,' she laughed.

'Am I not a Nigerian by birth?' asked Dr Saba. 'I have a Nigerian passport and I will see to it. If anybody questions my nationality then the Director is a member. No difficulty at all. We'll go back through the bar, which is just here.'

Actually the bar was open on one side overlooking the pool. Although it was very busy Debbie saw Marc Roland immediately. He was casually dressed in bush shirt and trousers, as though he had just dropped in for a drink on his way home, and he was talking to a lavender-haired lady and her bald-pated spouse.

'Ah, Miss Wyndham and Dr Saba!' he called. 'I don't suppose I can buy you a lemonade or something, Ranji?' he asked.

'No, thank you, Marc. I would be too tempted to ask you to put a gin in it, and that would be bad for both my liver and my conscience. Would you like a drink, Miss Wyndham?'

'Let me see to that,' Marc offered. 'Where's your party? I'll bring her back in ten minutes,' he told the young doctor, and held a chair for Debbie at a table for two. 'I believe the question is what's your poison?' he smiled at her. 'Campari? Very well.'

A steward brought two drinks and Marc looked at her expectantly. 'I got your note thanking me for the kippers,' he said. 'What did you mean by the rest of your message, nothing happening and that you didn't care?'

Debbie took a sip of the pink liquid in her glass and said, 'Well, it's true. I think this ennui you told me about has got me, too. I don't seem to be able to care. I keep thinking Jim and I are going to be exactly as we were, and when we're not I can't get in a state about it. It's as though I haven't the emotional energy to mind, and I'm now doing my full stint of work, you know. Perhaps I should give my emotions a rest for the six months I'm here.'

'That's the easy way out. I told you we all get this mental and emotional paralysis and it's something we have to fight and conquer.'

'Then if I conquer it on my own, where am I? My partner would probably still regard me as someone from another planet. Actually this ennui is rather pleasant. I mean, nothing hurts. It's preferable to the hell of banging one's head against a brick wall.'

'I don't agree. It's insidious and dangerous. One begins not to care how one looks, and then one's work suffers. I know mine did, and where you're working with human beings you can't afford to become slack.'

'Then what's the answer?' she demanded of him.

'The answer is that you and I have to have a public and blatant affair. We have to see a lot of each other, both publicly and privately. We even have to——'

She stared at him, startled.

'At least, that's what it's got to look like,' he said softly. 'If we manage to give Jim one hell of a bad time, then it will all have been worth it, and if he still doesn't respond, then nothing will be lost.'

'I never heard anything so outrageous in all my——'

'Hello!' Jim was now looming over them. 'Hello, Roland. I don't think we've actually met since that dinner party the Director gave about six months ago, have we?'

'No.' Marc rose and offered his hand. 'One understands you're always busy at the hospital. But now that you've decided to come to the Club we may meet more often.'

'Well, I haven't decided whether to join or not yet. This is Dr Saba's guest night,' and Jim laughed chummily. 'I don't know if I could stand much of it.'

'Our loss, if you don't,' Marc shrugged. 'Fortunately Miss Wyndham seems to find our company tolerable. She has just become a member.'

'Really?' asked Jim, while Debbie tried not to look aghast. 'I thought one had to be proposed, and all that?'

'Not the ladies, God bless 'em!' said Marc. 'There are too few of them for all that fandango.' He looked round the bar and beyond to the salon where a few couples danced lazily to soft music from a record-player. 'The ratio is about eight to one, would you agree?'

'I suppose so. But——'

'So Debbie is coming down for a swim on Saturday and will then meet many of our young members, the children. I'm sure she'd like that.'

'Would you, Debbie?' Jim asked, not looking one whit put out.

'A swim would be heaven,' she smiled. 'Thank you, Marc.'

'Then we'll make it dinner, maybe at my place. I have some veal in my deep-freeze. I raised it, so I hope it will be good.'

Jim said, 'Don't be long, Debbie. Sister's tired. She works hardest of us all, I think. Unless you'd like Mr Roland to bring you back?'

'No, of course I'm coming with you,' said Debbie.

'I'm still Dr Saba's guest.' She glared across at Marc Roland when Jim had left. 'I don't know whether to thank you or to say you have a damned cheek!' she said.

'Well, at least you've come out of your attack of ennui a little bit,' he smiled, and those devastating eyes of his actually twinkled. 'The die is cast, as they say. Somebody has to do something about you two.'

She rose without another word and left him, though she had to acknowledge Mary Tate apparently about to occupy the chair she had just vacated, by the smile on her pleasant face.

Standing in thoughtfully at Dr Oduloru's clinic, Debbie was still not used to her own somewhat chaotic private life. True to his word, Marc Roland was paying her a great deal of attention: he took her to the Club and they swam and shared drinks together so that everybody saw them, and she went to his house for an occasional meal, the invitation for which would be delivered publicly, and, as Jim had decided to join the Club, sometimes in his presence. Though people might wonder what happened when she met Marc in private, nothing did, save that they discussed Jim's reactions to their friendship, or lack of them.

'Oh,' Debbie had said on the last occasion she had been at Marc's, 'I told Jim I was coming here and he simply asked me if I'd like to borrow his car. He collected it last week, you know. When I told him you were sending transport for me he seemed quite cheerful, in fact he said in that case he'd run up to the Club and have dinner. He just doesn't care, Marc.'

'Well——' Marc said thoughtfully—'I'd rather like to carry on as we are doing, Debbie. I enjoy your company. We have the same sense of humour and, when you look back on all this, you're probably going to laugh about it all.'

'I'm afraid you're neglecting your other friends for

me. The Barhams——' this was the couple where the lady had lavender hair—'were saying quite pointedly that they haven't seen much of you lately, and they looked at me as they said it.'

'Well, we're eventually wanting Jim to say that to you, aren't we? And look at me as he says it.'

Debbie's answer was a long sigh. 'Anyway,' she said, 'I'm enjoying my work. What I do need is a car, an old banger would do. If I had wheels I'd be more independent.'

'I'll keep my eyes open for a car that bangs less than most. After a year of driving on these roads a Rolls could be called an old banger.'

Now the end of the queue was in sight, and Debbie noted in her book that she was to give arm exercises to a nine-year-old girl who had suffered a greenstick fracture at some point in her life and, without being properly reduced, the bones had overlapped and caused a shortening of the right arm, which was inclined to hang limp.

Debbie thought ahead to the evening when she was playing the hostess.

She had told Marc, 'Would you come to dinner next Tuesday at my wee house? I've already asked Mary.'

'Certainly. I'd be delighted. Do we dress?'

'Of course. We must keep the flag of empire flying. Oh, but it wasn't your empire, was it?'

'On my mother's side,' he reminded her, 'so it was half my empire, too. I'll uphold its traditions, don't worry.'

She had told Jim the previous evening. 'I've discovered Kadiri's an excellent cook. I give him his head and everything I've had so far has been delicious. I'm giving a dinner-party tomorrow. I've asked Marc and Mary Tate to come.'

'Am I invited?' Jim had asked teasingly.

'Well, if you'd like to come——'

'Of course I'd like to come. Thanks! I shall look forward to it.'

His eyes had been more alive than she remembered since her arrival and had made her wonder if some spark had at last been re-ignited in him. She had rushed forthwith to ask Sister to join the party, so that lady would not feel left out. Sister was getting ready for bed, but when she heard Debbie announce herself had opened her door readily. She was in a plain loose cotton dressing-gown, starkly white, and Debbie would have imagined Sister to be a nun apart from the fact that her black hair hung down over her shoulders, sleekly brushed out.

'Forgive me, Sister, for disturbing you so late, but I'm having a dinner party tomorrow in my wee house. Will you come? Jim, Marc Roland and Mary Tate are already invited.'

'Oh, what a pity!' Sister said quietly. 'I'm going up to the Thompsons'. It seems that Mrs Thompson used to be a nurse and I suppose that's the reason. Perhaps another time, Miss Wyndham? Anyhow, you'll have enough to cope with squeezing four adults round your table. Have I anything you'd like to borrow as I'll be out myself?'

'I think your cutlery's stronger than mine. My Okusha forks bend and the knives won't cut for toffee.'

'Right.' Sister rose dismissively from her chair on the veranda. 'I'll send Dawa down with them in the morning and I hope you have a lovely party.'

When told next morning that he had to cook for four people, Kadiri said, surprisingly, 'No can do.'

'What do you mean no can do? I've told everybody what a good cook you are.'

'I good cook,' Kadiri said modestly, 'but no can do. Oven too small. Missie buy cooker only for one people. Mebbe two people, but no can do for four.'

'What am I to do?' Debbie wailed. 'I've asked them

now, and they're all dressing up specially. Kadiri . . .?' she pleaded.

'Missie no worry. I t'ink of somet'ing. I got all day to t'ink.'

She had to go and do her work wondering what was happening. As she got ready that evening, there were no cooking smells, and only fleeting glimpses of Kadiri coming and going. Debbie wore a blue dress and looked, though she had no mirror to reflect the fact, lovely. The table was beautifully laid for four, with Sister's bone-handled cutlery and well-polished glasses, flowers arranged in a floral saucer made a pretty centrepiece, there were even sprigs of wild jasmine breathing out their sweetness.

Mary was the first to arrive. She was extremely petite and wore a dress which could have belonged to her mother, of tussore silk, obviously old but dainty and feminine. She was one of those people who genuinely couldn't do a thing with her hair; it was short and curled naturally all over her head. Mary swam at the Club without a cap, came out of the pool, shook her head like a small retriever and looked exactly the same as before. Once, as she had told Debbie, when she had taken to wearing slacks people had called her 'Mister', and as she was very much a female at heart she had parted with the slacks pretty quickly and never worn them since.

Kadiri floated in looking smart and important in his new white pyjama suit with the stand-up collar and brass buttons. He stood expectantly by the side-table where the drinks were set out.

'What will you have, Mary?' Debbie asked dutifully.

'Oh, South African sherry will do fine. Marc always says I have no palate or I would never drink sherry from anywhere but Jerez.'

'I don't think we can get Spanish sherry here,' Debbie said. She asked Kadiri out of the corner of her mouth, 'What's happening about dinner?'

'Missie have sherry, too?' he asked normally, then answered similarly. 'No to worry. All taken care of.'

Debbie decided to take Mary into her confidence just in case anything went wrong. 'As you see, I have hardly room to swing a cat here, and it appears my cooker's on the small side, too. My boy says "no can cook for four" on it, so we may have cold cuts and a salad. I've had to leave things to him.'

'Who cares about the eats at these do's, apart from the hostess?' Mary replied. 'The main thing we come for is the chat and just to be wholly European for a change. In maintaining the cultures of the people we educate, it's also important, I think, to guard our own. We can never become Nigerians, or listen to the drums with the same rapture we reserve for Beethoven, Chopin, or even Cole Porter, come to that——'

'Yes, I see what you mean,' Debbie said. 'When we're together we can just be ourselves, maybe even discuss the weather?'

'That's sure to come into it,' and Mary laughed. She was still laughing as Jim arrived and they shook hands.

Jim looked very smart in black trousers, a white silk dinner jacket, and black bow tie and Debbie felt proud and warmed towards him. His hair was thick and leonine and tawny, and his eyes like damp sand, but he was obviously in a very good mood and seemed set to enjoy himself. He told Kadiri he would have a whisky and soda and asked Mary how her new side stroke was coming along.

'Have you seen him swim?' Mary asked. Debbie said she hadn't, actually. She didn't believe he could.

'Oh, yes,' Mary assured the other, while Jim still smiled, 'but he can only swim on his side. However he starts off he finishes on his side, and he offered to show me how it was done. I, who have been swimming since I was two and have a dozen medals to prove it! But I'm always willing to learn anything new.'

'But you couldn't do it,' teased Jim. 'However you

started off you always finished up on either your tummy or your back.'

'I agree it's an art,' Mary smiled back.

Debbie was glad all was going so well and wished Marc would hurry up to complete the party. Half an hour later she was feeling rather desperate and Kadiri's questioning face appearing round the kitchen door didn't help. Once he whispered to her, 'No good soon. Everythin' spoil.'

'We'll give Mr Roland another quarter of an hour,' Debbie said, 'then we'll start without him.'

Kadiri looked at the red plastic watch he had bought on the strength of having a new job and said severely, 'When him say half-past, me say "dinner is served". O.K.?'

Debbie almost gushed as she heard Marc's footsteps on the gravel path Kadiri had made to her door. She said, 'I was beginning to think you couldn't make it.' Under the porch light she looked up into those brilliant-blue eyes, took in his smoothly-brushed black hair, *his* evening clothes, which seemed to fit even better than Jim's did, and his cummerbund was certainly neater and tighter and her heart did a peculiar turn over in her chest. From behind his back he produced a bunch of pink rosebuds and said, 'Sweets to the sweet. They won't last a day, but that's not the point, is it?'

Then they were inside with the others and everybody was saying hello and only Debbie found herself still feeling odd, as though she was incubating the symptoms which would inconvenience her tomorrow. Marc now had a drink in his hand and was apologising for being late.

'We had a birthday,' he announced. 'Any midwife will tell you such things always happen when one has firm plans to do something else. A mare usually drops her foal with little trouble, but cows sometimes have complications and my breeding bulls are big chaps and can produce large calves. Anyway, all is now well and we have a lovely yellow and white heifer calf, already named Debbie,' and he raised his glass and drank to his hostess.

'How's Mary coming along?' asked the other Mary, as though to tell Debbie that Marc had a habit of calling female calves after his girl-friends.

'Giving me trouble, just as you do.' A glance flashed between the friends and Debbie noticed that Mary had coloured up slightly.

'Dinner is served,' Kadiri appeared to announce, though the guests still had to sit at table.

Marc said, 'Shall I be wine-waiter?' and began to deal with a bottle of chilled hock while Kadiri served what Debbie thought were shrimps in aspic, but turned out to be small crayfish, and were quite delicious.

That was the last they saw of Kadiri for quite some time, for suddenly a couple of strange young boys took over and Debbie saw Dawa hovering in the kitchen door. After smelling nothing, suddenly delicious smells coming from the kitchen made everybody's gastric juices run. Dishes of peas and green beans and baked yams appeared on the side-table and Dawa himself came in with plates of roast pork, swimming in gravy and each portion with a piece of dark brown crackling.

'Where's Kadiri?' Debbie managed to ask.

'Mohammedans not touch pig,' Dawa said. 'He be back. We all Christians. These my brothers.'

'What an absolutely gorgeous meal!' sighed Mary, who had originally only come for the chat and a little European culture. 'Roast baby pig! I don't know when I had it last.'

Every plate was soon empty and both men had second helpings of meat. Eventually Kadiri reappeared with a bowl of fresh fruit and the coffee. The hirelings had washed up the contaminated plates and taken the remainder of the meat with them and he now felt his kitchen to be safe for him to take over once more.

Marc asked if he might light a pipe and Debbie felt

that odd sensation in her chest once more as he lit it and the match-flame reflected in his eyes. Even Jim, who hardly smoked at all, produced a thin cigar and the heavy air was soon blue with smoke, as Debbie had no fan, but was very fragrant. Everybody looked quite happy and contented and the hostess considered the evening to have been quite a success and the unexpected meal especially delicious.

'By the way,' Marc said suddenly, 'I think I've got you some wheels, Debbie.'

'Wheels?' she asked blankly.

'Yes. You said you wanted your own car, remember?'

'Not worth her buying a car for a few months,' Jim demurred. 'I've told Debbie she can always borrow mine.'

'Yes, but if you happen to want to go to A, and Debbie wants to go to B——' Marc took a long puff on his pipe and then shrugged. 'Anyway, no money's involved. The Davieses live near Arusha, and they're going home on leave. They have a jeep, and rather than keep it in the garage they asked me to take it over. I think Debbie could keep it exercised and I mentioned her need to them. They're quite happy for her to have it. It's a left-hand drive, so I suggest we go on Saturday, Debbie, and you can get some practice by driving it back with me as trail blazer in the Land-Rover. O.K.?'

'I don't think we had any special plans for Saturday, had we?' Debbie deferred to Jim.

'No. It's Sister's birthday and I've invited her to the Club, and I can try to teach Mary to swim on her side in the afternoon,' and he laughed.

'Better I teach you the conventional ways of swimming,' Mary said. 'So you two will be gone almost forty-eight hours,' she added conversationally, looking from Marc to Debbie.

'Yes. The Davieses will probably put us up, but if not there's the rest-house,' said Marc.

'I've got to be going,' Mary suddenly announced, and Debbie wondered if she was in any way upset. 'I can't keep late nights.'

Marc said, 'I'll see you to your car, Mary,' and off they went.

'Nice girl that,' said Jim, coming to the end of his cigar and stubbing it out in an ash tray.

'Yes, she's very nice.'

'I wonder nobody's snapped her up. I mean, there aren't that many good-looking girls around.'

'Sometimes people presume that a girl must be "snapped up" and don't get around to asking her,' Debbie commented.

'Well, she's been asked, believe me,' Jim told her. 'She's known men in her time.'

'Maybe not the right one, though,' said Debbie, and as Marc returned they dropped the subject.

'Well——?' he held out a hand to Debbie and clasped hers warmly. 'A really pleasant evening. But I too must go. Can you be ready by eight a.m. on Saturday? We have a long drive.'

'Of course.' Jim stood behind her slightly as they watched Marc stride off in the direction of the tennis court, the hospital and his parked car. She half turned, bumped into Jim and apologised.

'What's a bump between old sweethearts?' he asked gently, and stooped and kissed her on the lips. 'Goodnight, love. Splendid evening.'

He wandered off as she put a hand to her lips and then in a gesture wiped away that kiss. Weeks ago she would have welcomed such an approach by Jim, have thrown her arms round his neck and done her best to fan that flicker into a blazing flame.

But her heart was somehow no longer in the project. She didn't want to renew anything that had once been between herself and Jim. She was very much afraid that something was happening over which she had no control. It was Marc Roland's attentions which were now becoming important to her. Every time she saw him her heart leapt, and tonight it had almost jumped out of her chest. The problem was that she and Marc had started out by playing a game, and to him their association was still probably only a game. He had left earlier than Jim, probably to be discreet and leave them—the ex-sweethearts—alone together. But her heart had gone with him, and now she felt peculiarly empty, and not only empty but afraid. She longed for Saturday to come and yet there was a dread in her longing.

It was in the early hours of the morning before at length she slept.

CHAPTER NINE

THE next morning Debbie was reluctant to leave dreamland and felt tired and a little depressed, but Kadiri, with her morning tea, brought his shining face to ask what her guests had thought about the dinner.

'Ah, yes,' she said, sipping the tea as the lad threw open the louvred shutters, 'how did you manage that gorgeous meal? What had Dawa to do with it?'

'It was all Dawa's idea. He my good friend now, you know. When he know what trouble I got he say no bother for him to cook in Dr Brant's kitchen, and that Christian folk like—like pig.' Kadiri couldn't conceal a grimace. 'He buy, and he cook and he serve. I no touch. Was good?'

'Very good. But I must owe somebody some money.'

'No, no. I pay for pig out of housekeeping and Dawa and brothers say they my friend, no pay friend. I do some time good thing for them.'

The day passed, and Jim seemed to have acquired a

sparkle which hadn't been there for ages. When he met her eyes he looked knowing, and smiled. The week passed and on the Friday evening he said to her, 'Now watch it this weekend. Don't do anything I wouldn't do.'

'What wouldn't you do?' she asked, trying to be as gay as he seemed to be.

'Well, I wouldn't—I don't know, though. I might.' He winked and chucked her under the chin. 'Watch that left-hand drive, now. It can be tricky the first time.'

'And don't let Mary drown you,' she countered. 'Is it true you can only swim on your side?'

'No. But don't tell Mary. It would spoil her fun.'

'Would you—tomorrow——' she felt in her pocket and pulled out a small packet—'give this to Sister? It's only a few hankies, but Okusha hasn't exactly got a Bond Street.'

'I'm sure Eve will be delighted. See you anon, then.'

He either trusts me or he doesn't really care, thought Debbie. She thought the morning would never dawn, and at times wished it wouldn't.

Promptly at a quarter to eight in the morning she was ready and as her transport arrived early she was at Marc's exactly on the hour. He seemed to be brisk and businesslike and she remembered in some confusion pressing one of the pink rosebuds he had brought her before it could have a chance to die. Any romantic notions were on her side only, and she mutely rebuked herself. She had come out here to work and be with Jim. Well, she *was* with Jim—though in a way not quite up to her expectations—and she had her work. Why couldn't she be content? Why had she to experience that many-splendoured thing called love as a background to the other events of her life?

'A niara for them,' said Marc suddenly, overtaking a mammy-wagon once he saw that the road ahead was clear.

'Sorry?' Debbie had almost jumped.

'Well, ten niaras, then. For your thoughts,' he encouraged.

'Oh, I'm sure they weren't worth anything. I can't even remember,' she lied.

'The calf died last night,' he said.

'The calf? You mean the one named after me? Oh, Marc!' and her eyes filled unaccountably with tears. 'What was wrong?'

'Its mum had a fever. Couldn't produce milk. We put the calf to another cow, but it wouldn't suck. We even tried the bottle—no good. It was just one of those things. Nobody's job goes right all the time.'

'Of course you must be disappointed and upset. You've probably been up half the night.'

'I had a visitor earlier last evening, all right and proper. She wrote a note and sent her steward round asking if it would be convenient for her to call. She shared my supper table, and the lady in question was— Sister Meadows.'

Debbie looked at him sharply. 'Why are you telling me?'

'Because I thought you ought to know. At least our apparent preference for one another's company has been noted in that quarter. Sister asked if I was aware that when you came out here you were engaged to Dr Brant. I said that I was but I understood the engagement was ended by mutual consent. By the time we reached the dessert stage she was telling me that providing there were no foolish distractions, the engagement would be on again in no time, and that she would be obliged if I would drop out of the picture and amuse myself somewhere else, as I was not without experience in that direction, and she proceeded to peel a banana as though she had just been commenting on the weather.'

'I can see her,' Debbie said. 'She never shows any emotion. If she was offering one a cup of hemlock she would say, "Just take that", and not turn a hair.'

'I did manage to poke a nerve eventually,' said Marc. 'I asked her if she had come as an ambassador from Dr Brant to ask me to leave his girl alone, and she replied no, he knew nothing of her visit and was not to know. She would not have him upset in any way. I then asked if she was in love with him, and she turned a dull red from the throat upwards and lost her cool a bit. How dare I! she spluttered. How could I! Then she collected her wits and said that such as I couldn't be expected to know that there was love and love, that my sort of love always ended up in bed with somebody, but that there was the love that was content to serve a man doing his job well, that desired only his complete happiness for its fulfilment. In this way she loved Jim Brant, but not sexually—here a shudder—though she realised that men had to satisfy their appetites as it was the way they were made. She sounded so superior that I told her women did, too, or, at least, most women, and that love could be total, and dedicated, *and* include sex. She said—back now to sweet reasonableness—that she had no more to say; if I wanted to go around breaking things up between people then that was my concern and I would have to live with the consequences. I said I would like to see Jim putting up the arguments she was putting, only more physically, and had she noticed him pining? No, she said, but he wouldn't show such things, he was very good at hiding his true feelings. I said she could say that again, and on that note we parted.'

'In some ways I'll be glad when I get away from here,' Debbie remarked. 'That woman watching me gives me the creeps. And my rôle, in her book, is merely to satisfy Jim's baser appetites while she supplies the true and shining comradely love.'

'How *are* Jim's appetites?' Marc inquired. 'Base or otherwise, is there an improvement between you?'

'No,' Debbie said flatly. 'He's jollier, nicer, but as

much in love with me as a cold pudding. I think he's quite happy with the status quo, and I wish Sister would mind her own business.'

'Please don't tell her I confided in you. I promised her I wouldn't inform Jim, and I think it was tacitly understood that our conversation was private. I only told you so that you could decide if we're to carry on with our charade. Obviously people are noticing, if only the wrong people, and I wouldn't want anybody to get really hurt.'

'You mean Jim may be bleeding quietly to death because of us?'

'I'm not only thinking of Jim.'

'Oh! You imagine *I* may really kid myself into thinking I'm in love with you, and join the queue, only to have to be kicked in the teeth at the end of it? Well, Mr desirable Roland, you have a nerve, I must say! You really think you're the Casanova of Okusha, don't you? Even old women simper and purr over you at the Club. It makes me sick! Well, you can forget it. Forget it, do you hear? When I get this car, thanks to you, I'll be independent of the lot of you. I can honestly live without you, so don't worry about me!'

There was absolute silence in the Land-Rover after her heavy breathing had eased. They were following the course of the river now, and it kept coming into sight, three-quarters of a mile wide at some points.

'As a matter of fact,' Marc said, fully fifteen minutes after her outburst, 'I was not concerned that you might be falling in love with me. That hadn't crossed my mind. I do not have an exaggerated opinion of my powers over females and I don't think old women at the Club either simper or purr over me. If they have any regard for me it's probably because I've neutered their cats or given their doggies Epivax injections.'

Debbie thought if she opened her mouth again it would only be to put her foot in it further, and so she remained silent. They stopped at one o'clock for lunch—Marc had brought a hamper—and they drank iced coffee and ate sandwiches in the shade of a rapture of tulip trees. Debbie thought that a very good collective noun as she looked up at the pink—striped with purple—blossoms, so very like tulips. For more than an hour not a single word had been exchanged, and at last Debbie broke the silence.

'I'm sorry, as usual,' she said, and tried a light laugh which didn't ring true.

'That's all right. Feel free to speak your mind any time.'

'My father always accused me of speaking first and thinking afterwards.'

'You were obviously Daddy's girl.'

They went on, and on and on and on.

'Can I relieve you?' she asked once.

'Better not. You'll be doing your share of driving all the way back. Another half hour and we'll be there.'

She glanced at her watch. 'You've made good time,' she said.

'Yes. We could get a couple of hours' driving in before dark and spend the night at the Umgoro Rest House.'

'As you wish.' She wouldn't have argued with him if he had announced that they were going over Victoria Falls in a barrel.

The Davieses were busy packing up and seemed relieved that the visitors wanted to stay no longer than it took to have a refreshing drink, fuel both vehicles and top them up with water and then start back.

'I'll look after the jeep, and thanks,' said Debbie.

'Have a good furlough,' Marc wished.

'Give Mary my love,' said Eileen Davies to Marc. 'I'm a bit peeved you didn't bring her to our anniversary party, but you probably had other fish to fry. Goodbye!'

The Land-Rover led and Debbie followed in the jeep, feeling a bit awkward sitting on the left-hand side and having to change gear with her right hand instead of her left, but she soon got the hang of it and Marc was only travelling at about thirty miles an hour, and she could see his reflection in his rear-view mirror, watching her progress.

Just how close were he and Mary? she wondered at one point. Mrs Davies had linked their names quite naturally and a girl who was free to take breakfast with a man on his veranda was obviously no stranger to him. Could he have meant that Mary might get hurt?

He sounded his horn sharply and she jumped to attention. A big Mercedes was hankering to pass. She dropped speed, allowed Marc to draw ahead and then waved the big car on. At half past six the light became peculiarly metallic and she knew that at any moment darkness could drop like a cloak, so she took the precaution of putting her lights on. Marc switched his on and off, on and off again, so Debbie took the hint and dowsed hers too. A moment later his left indicator flickered and he turned off down a track in the forest. She followed, sweating from the concentration of handling a strange vehicle and feeling peculiarly pummelled from the day's exchanges.

The two vehicles arrived in a clearing where there stood a long, low house which had once been white-washed but was now grubby and peeling. It had a wide veranda with the rail broken in two places and the inevitable corrugated iron roof.

'Not exactly Claridges,' said Marc, 'but it'll do.'

An old man came on bent, bowed legs, showing stumps of decaying teeth in a broad grin. Marc addressed him in dialect and the fellow disappeared round the back. He reappeared carrying linen and a storm-lantern, for it was now almost dark, and indicated that they follow him. He fussed about in a cobweb-hung room, putting musty-smelling mattresses on the two beds and making them up.

'He obviously believes us to be married,' said Marc,

'and as I don't understand much of his dialect I can't put him wise. But don't worry. When he's gone, after supper I'll sleep in the car.'

'Did you say supper?' Debbie asked, thinking that the hollowness she felt must be hunger.

'Yes. I've got some meat and salad in the cool-box and he's making us a pot of tea. Will you settle for that?'

'That sounds fine.'

They ate outside in a kind of picnic area, beset by insects of all kinds but which one learnt to ignore after a while. The tea the old man produced tasted of smoke, as the water had been boiled over an open fire, but with tinned milk it was quite refreshing. Half a moon, like a slice of melon, sailed overhead.

'He's definitely Semitic,' Debbie commented, waving a large moth away from the attraction of the lamp in the middle of the rough wooden table.

'Who? The moth?'

'No,' Debbie laughed, 'I meant the man in the moon. Just look at that great hooked nose of his!'

'My mother used to recite a nursery rhyme to me, "The man in the moon came down too soon—"'

'"And asked his way to Norwich",' Debbie continued. 'I don't know any more only that he ate cold plum porridge. I don't suppose there *is* a better rhyme for Norwich? Why couldn't he have gone to Dover?'

'Oh, what profundities!' grinned Marc. 'Did you ever imagine you'd be sitting outside an African Government rest-house, bitten to death by various bugs and watched by a Semitic African moon whose mythical occupant preferred Norwich to Dover?'

'No, I can't say I ever did. In those days when I dreamed dreams I used to picture myself lying on a deserted tropical beach, and Mr Universe coming out of the palms to meet me. There were never any bugs of any description.'

'Well?' Marc stifled a yawn. 'We'd better get some

sleep, I suppose. I'll see you to the bedroom and collect a blanket, if you don't mind. You keep the lamp. I've got a torch in the car if I need it.'

Together they went up the steps into the rest-house, carrying the storm-lantern. One of the steps creaked and Marc warned, 'Watch out! It must be riddled with termites.' Debbie discovered she was next to a sort of bathroom which had no door or plug in the bath, but cold water did run after a trickle of rust had preceded it.

'It must be ages since anybody last stayed here,' she told Marc.

'Can you wonder? Anyway, it's a bed, or rather two beds, and a roof.' He had a grey blanket under his arm. 'Goodnight,' he said in the doorway, met her eyes briefly as she responded and disappeared.

She cleaned her teeth and washed her hands and face, but didn't attempt serious ablutions because of that missing door, though she was sure there was nobody to see within miles, only Marc in the Land-Rover and the old man in his hut at the back of the rear compound. In any case, there were no towels and she had to dry herself on a handkerchief.

Back in the bedroom she took off her blue bush-suit; Mary had told her where to get them made and they were very smart and practical consisting of a nicely-tailored jacket, with patch-pockets, a belt and a gored skirt, worn with knee-length white cotton hose and snake-boots, which were really called anti-snake boots and came to just above the ankle. She had two such suits and felt comfortable in them. Their greatest virtue was that they were washable, which everything had to be in this climate.

She was down to her petticoat when she sat on one of the beds to remove her boots. She saw what she thought was a pretty black and white pebble on the broken cement floor and reached down to examine it more closely, when it suddenly took off and she realised it was a jumping spider. Jim had told her about them, and they were not dangerous, but actually coming upon one in those circumstances made her catch her breath. She decided her best place was between the sheets and well tucked in, though it was unlikely the spider would seek her out as it was probably terrified, too. Deciding to sleep just as she was, she pulled down the sheet. After a moment her screams rent the air. She yelled 'Marc! Marc!' and ran to meet him, falling into his arms as he was racing up the steps. When she could speak she stuttered, 'A—a snake—in the bed! I don't want to go back in there.'

'We must,' he said. The old man had now appeared and was obviously asking what was the matter. Marc made some response and the fellow disappeared into the bedroom. There was the sound of banging and he emerged triumphantly carrying a limp green body in his hand.

'Now sleep tight,' he said with a grin, an expression he must have picked up from English visitors, and went off to his quarters.

'Come on!' said Marc, drawing Debbie after him. 'I'll have a good look round. It was only a harmless grass snake.'

'There was a jumping spider, too,' Debbie said.

'Well, they're rather nice little fellows when you get to know them. Come on, get into bed.'

She crept between the sheets while he carefully investigated below the beds and in all the corners.

'You'll be O.K. now,' he said. 'Leave the lamp burning.'

'No, I—please don't go.'

He looked at her and noted her pallor. She had really had quite a fright. 'O.K.,' he said, sitting down on the other bed. 'I'll stay, but in that case we'll put the light out.'

Fifteen minutes later she called, 'Marc, are you awake?'

'Yes. What is it?'

'I know I'm stupid, but I can't get warm. Some sort of shock, I expect.'

'I'll come and cuddle up to you. Now you're not to worry about a thing.' In the darkness he drew her to him, noting her chill, and pressing his warm body close to her. She was tremendously comforted, but because she was not a child and he was not a favourite uncle there came the time when their closeness brought other feelings into play. She moved her head and found his lips, her own trembled and his were strong as steel as they pressed, sending her temperature as suddenly skyhigh as it had previously dropped. She was aware of other areas of reaction, of her limbs that stirred against his and the hard masculinity of his stomach close to hers. He said in an odd, tight voice, 'I think we'd better go to sleep. I'll leave you now.'

She kissed his ear and hung on to him.

'We're playing with fire, Deborah.'

It was the first time he had used her full name and she thought it had never sounded sweeter, slightly French and nasal.

'I don't seem to care. Do you, Jean-Marc?'

The Semitic moon glanced idly through the bars of the window and appeared to grin. Maybe a cow had just jumped over him or he had called in at Norwich for his plum porridge. He edged away and eventually sank into the Atlantic, and shortly afterwards Debbie awoke to a grey and ghostly African morning. She was alone and looked round as though fearing that she had only been dreaming. But on the other bed the pillow was still dented from Jean-Marc's head and on her own pillow, where his had lain for the moments that now seemed eternity, was a single, yellow orchid-type flower with a red tongue.

She put the flower to her lips and swung her feet to the floor, giving not a thought to either snakes or spiders. Marc came into the room carrying a cup of tea.

'Here,' he said. 'I don't think it's smoked. I made it myself.'

'Thank you, darling.' She jumped up to hug him.

'No, no,' he said forbiddingly. 'No more of that, young lady! You have to drive back to Okusha, remember? And anyway, we have to have a serious talk, you and I. A *very* serious talk.'

'Yes, darling,' and she smiled.

'I'm not joking,' he told her, and frowned to show her how serious it all was. 'Now drink that tea. We have to make an early start.'

She grimaced after him as he left because she felt so happy, happier than she had been since arriving on this continent, and he was just being a bit standoffish because he couldn't bear to be so close with her again only to have to break apart, as they had broken last night, with her arms still reaching for him.

'You're a witch,' had been his pronouncement on that occasion. 'Now be good and go to sleep.'

CHAPTER TEN

JIM asked, 'Anything wrong with it?'

Debbie poked the roast guinea-fowl and vegetables on her plate and said, 'No. But suddenly I'm not a bit hungry. That's funny, because earlier I was absolutely ravenous. Mary's just come in with the Barhams. I don't think she's seen us.'

Jim twisted round and then Mary twinkled her fingers as she sat down at a distant table.

'She's a great sport, is Mary,' Jim confided, as he returned her salute. 'I never knew a woman with such a sense of humour.'

'Did Sister enjoy her birthday party?' Debbie asked, forcing a mouthful of the fowl down.

'Oh, you know Eve. She said fancy such nonsense as celebrating birthdays one preferred to forget! She can't be that old.'

'I happen to know she's twenty-six,' Debbie said, 'and she's not exactly doddering towards decrepitude. She's the sort of woman who'll still be absolutely beautiful at forty, and beyond.'

'That's a very generous thing for one woman to say about another,' Jim said approvingly.

'Good gracious!' Debbie looked surprised. 'All women aren't bitchy about each other. Sister *is* beautiful, Mary Tate is cute and intelligent and I should imagine absolutely honest. Now what they would say about me, I don't know, but I have merely stated the facts as I see them.'

'You're very pretty, too, Debbie.'

'Well, thank you.' The compliment somehow left her cold where once it would have thrilled her. She even felt physically cold and shivered. 'I'm sorry, Jim, but I can't seem to be able to eat.'

He looked at her and now her eyes were brilliant and she put a hand to her head.

'I'm awfully hot.' She threw her evening shawl from her shoulders and then snatched it up again as another shiver shook her. 'Now I'm cold. Oh, God, the room's spinning round!'

'Debbie,' Jim's voice came as through a fog, she couldn't actually see him, 'have you been taking your proquanil regularly?'

She surfaced to regard him in another blaze of heat.

'I don't think I have, not for about five days. Now I've got the most awful stomach cramps. What's wrong with me, Jim?'

'You little fool! You've probably got malaria. We must get back and let Iloro have a look at you. Really, Debbie, prevention is much better than cure. You can surely take a tablet when you're told! Now look at the inconvenience you're causing everybody!'

The rest was all a jumble in her mind, voices in the Club as people helped Jim to get her into the car, and shuddering rigors which left her exhausted and then fevers which brought delirium. She was not aware of being put to bed in a side-ward at the hospital, of the straps which restrained her when her inclination was to thresh about and throw off all the bedclothes, of Dr Iloro's deep African eyes or his hands pulling down the lids to examine her own, and the chloro-quinine injections and Sister herself, who insisted on washing away the perspiration which poured from her and changing her gown and bedclothes with the tirelessness of a saint as the fever took its course. In a way she was nothing, a piece of driftwood borne along on the current of events, but she was an unhappy nothing, like a ghost in limbo, not knowing to which element it now belongs, and it was with a frightened scream that she eventually surfaced from this limbo to behold Sister's pale eyes quietly regarding her.

'Oh, so you're with us again, Miss Wyndham.' Cool fingers on her brow. 'That's much, much better.'

'Where have I been?' Debbie's voice sounded like gravel coming through a sieve and Sister put the spout of a feeding cup to her lips which contained lemonade sweetened with glucose.

'There and back again,' Sister smiled. 'No need to worry. It's all over now.'

'How—long?' Oh, what an effort to put two words together!

'A week. A nasty attack, but Dr Iloro doesn't think it will recur. Your spleen may be enlarged, but one can live with that.'

'A—a—week?' Debbie had an idea she should worry about something, but already her lids were leaden.

'That's right,' came Sister's voice approvingly. 'Have a good sleep. Nobody will disturb you,' but Debbie was already in the arms of Morpheus and didn't hear a thing.

The next time she came round she felt much stronger and able to take an interest in her surroundings. Mentally she was normal though her legs still felt leaden. The side-ward resembled Kew Gardens, there were so many flowers, and when Sister called in and looked approvingly on her patient Debbie thought it was safe to ask a few questions.

'Has anyone enquired after me?' she wanted to know.

'Why,' Sister smiled and indicated the flowers, 'just about the world and his wife. I didn't know you'd got to know so many people. Of course everybody at the Club that night you were taken ill has asked after you. I don't know who sent all these—many were just left at the office by stewards—but Dr Brant did buy that pot-plant there, with the purple flower. You can take that back to your house with you and it likes a drink every night. Are you up to reading your mail?'

'Yes, certainly,' and Debbie's heart leapt, wondering if *he* had written. Sister didn't come back, but a nurse called in holding a bundle fastened by an elastic band. A couple of items were air-mail letters from England, and were from her mother and Elsa, two were unstamped, so obviously local, and one *had* to be from Marc—she willed it. The rest were magazines and brochures.

As, when a child, she had always kept the treat of eating her meat to the end, faithfully demolishing hated vegetables first, so now she kept what she was sure was Marc's letter to the end. She read her mother's letter first, not as a hated vegetable but because she genuinely wanted to know that all was well on the home front. Winter had really set in, said her mother, with temperatures being recorded which were the lowest for fifty years in parts. Jill had had 'flu, but was feeling better now. She had a new boy-friend, Mike Mahill, who seemed very nice and suitable, but Debbie knew what Jill was like, so hard to please.

'Aren't we all, Mum, in the event?' Debbie asked quietly. 'I agree that Jill should hang on and wait for the real thing. She'll know when it arrives.'

Elsa wrote of her wrangles with Pam, her new flat-mate. 'She makes you seem like a saint,' she remarked. 'We have a new senior radiologist with a very fine moustache. She's a real old cow!'

Debbie smiled that the owner of the fine moustache turned out to be a woman, and then slit open the first of the local letters. It was from Mary and was brief and to the point.

Dear Debbie,

I was so sorry to hear you had malaria. I had been on the point of asking you to come and sample my cooking, as I think it's time we got together and had a natter. So as soon as you're fit enough we must meet.

Hoping you're not feeling too rotten.

Mary.

At long, long last Debbie opened her final letter, and when it began 'Dear Miss Wyndham', her eyes flew to the signature at the end and it was signed 'Simon Ungaro', who was Marc's assistant.

She started to read again:

Dear Miss Wyndham,

Marc has asked me to inform you that Wednesday is off. You will understand what he means by that. I am to explain that on his return, a telegram was awaiting summoning him to Lagos pronto. He drove off hoping to catch a plane from Jos, which would shorten travelling time considerably. I am sure he will be in touch on his return.

Very sincerely yours,
Simon Ungaro.

'So he doesn't even know I've been ill,' Debbie

pondered a bit miserably, 'and he can't be back or he'd
have heard.'

A little later on Kadiri was allowed in to see her,
and she asked him to find out if Master Roland was
home yet or not.

'He not,' Kadiri said confidently. 'He gone get drugs
for cattle and such. Last lot done get stole by bad mens
between here and Lagos. Sell on black market, I t'ink.'

'Oh, I see.' Debbie decided this would give her time
to really get better, for on trying out her legs she had
discovered a mirror and was horrified to see her yellow
countenance. Even the whites of her eyes were yellow.

Thus it was that when she was eventually sent to
convalesce in her own house, Mary Tate was her first
visitor. Mary made them both an omelette, seasoned
with herbs, which Kadiri served.

'There!' said Mary. 'That's nice and light. I do hope
you don't mind me descending on you like this,
Debbie, but I wanted to get this chat over before Marc
gets back.'

'Oh?' Debbie was now watchful and wary. 'Is it
about Marc you wish to speak?'

'Only in part. I want to talk about Marc and Jim,
you and me.'

'Oh?' Debbie asked again. 'In what context?'

'Well, I make it sound as though we're two couples,
don't I?' Mary seemed to be eating her omelette with
undiminished appetite. 'But we're not, are we? I mean,
you seem to have them both eating out of your hand
and I—I——' at last Mary looked confused and put
down her fork—'I try not to mind, but I do. I'm hurt.
Oh, forgive me! People must have thought old Mary
was beyond falling in love at her age, but I'm not. I've
proved it. I have this chance to go and take full charge
of a girls' school in Kenya, and I'd take it like a shot if
I thought I hadn't any chance with him. But I've got
to know what you intend to do. I don't mean I want
you to hand him over to me on a plate, but if you're

just playing around—well, say so, and if you think it could be serious, then tell me that, too. The one thing a girl can keep is her dignity in these matters. He may not care two hoots for me and I could still finish up in Kenya, but I'm not going to compete for him. He's kind to me always, and we enjoy being together, but the time's coming when I'm going to want more than kindness, and when I see him with you I feel I—I could hate you. Debbie, I'm sorry. I'm doing this very badly.'

'No, on the contrary I think you've made things very plain, Mary.' Both had now lost all interest in the omelettes, which Kadiri swiftly removed, no doubt having designs on them for himself. Debbie remembered how Marc had said, 'Obviously people are noticing, if only the wrong people, and I wouldn't want anybody to get really hurt.' She had responded, 'You mean Jim maybe bleeding quietly to death because of us?'

'I'm not only thinking of Jim,' Marc had said, and now Debbie fancied she had stumbled on the truth. Marc did not relish the idea of hurting Mary, his friend of such long standing. Maybe he suspected the tenderness of her feelings for him and maybe, had Debbie not come along, he would have grown to reciprocate. The idea of Mary going off to Kenya, to get away from the unhappiness of unrequited passion, was something Debbie felt unable to live with. So far as she knew she hadn't hurt anybody in her life and she didn't intend to start now.

'You know, Mary,' she managed a light laugh as Kadiri served the coffee, 'when people fall in love they see everybody else as being in the same plight as themselves. You go right ahead and stop thinking of me as competition. I'm not. I'm only here temporarily and I certainly don't want to leave a trail of blight behind me, like a tornado. You haven't to compete with me for anybody, so just go ahead and—and God bless you both!'

'Oh, Debbie, you're sure?'

'I'm sure.'

Mary actually gave a self-conscious little laugh that had tears in it. 'Of course, he may not fancy me as a life partner. We'll just have to wait and see, won't we? I do know he likes me.'

'That's a good start,' Debbie smiled, wondering whom she was to speak with the voice of experience. 'Sometimes people get married who don't actually like each other, and that can lead to trouble.'

'Well, I won't stay. You're looking tired and must have an early night. I hope you'll soon be feeling A.1.'

Dr Iloro had told Debbie that she might suffer a period of depression, but that this was normal and she mustn't worry about it. But as Debbie drew out writing materials and sat at the table by the light of the lamp, she felt such a weight in her chest that she thought it must surely be a physical malady she was suffering, from which she might well die at any minute, but that firstly she had something to do.

Dear Marc, (she wrote)

I know that you will be unaware that I went down with malaria the day we got back with the jeep, and so for ten days I've been out of circulation. Being so has enabled me to review certain events between us, and I now think I must have been starting my illness when I behaved so heedlessly in the rest-house with you, and may have given you grounds to believe that I was being serious. I received your message, via Simon, but there's really nothing more to discuss and I hope we can put the whole thing out of our minds. If we do meet, by accident, then I hope we can be civilised about it.

Yours very sincerely,
Deborah.

'Sleep on it,' her instinct told her, but she refused to

listen to instinct and addressed an envelope without more ado.

'Kadiri!' she called.

He came, his hands wet with suds.

'You call me, missie?'

'Yes. I want you to take this letter to Master Roland's house.'

'But he not back yet, and I wash up.'

'I want it to be there when he does get back, and leave the washing up. Take the letter. Is important,' she added.

'Aw right, I take letter. You hear drums, missie?'

She tried to notice the physical world about her and heard the drums, indeed. They sounded every evening and blended into the background of the bush and the smells and the dark, steamy air of night.

'Yes, I hear them,' she said blankly.

'Well, they say Master Roland coming back. I take letter quick.'

'Kadiri——' she stayed him—'you mean the drums actually tell things to people?'

'Not long ago all Africa speak with drum. Much more quicker than telegram or letter. Kadiri best damn drummer in village. You hear him some time.'

'Yes, yes, I will. But now, the letter, eh?'

'I going,' and snatching his woolly cap from a nail on the wall, he went.

The drums must have been right, for next morning Kadiri brought a reply to her letter and this time in the gothic type of script she knew was Jean-Marc's. She tore open the envelope nervously.

Dear Debbie, (the letter began)

You've got to be kidding. Malaria does funny things to people, but not *that*. Obviously you're not quite out of the wood yet, but in a couple or so days we've got to talk. It's surely only civilised (your word) that you tell me to get lost in person, if you really do mean it?

Please tell my messenger when it would be convenient for me to come and see you.

Marc.

The messenger was waiting with Kadiri in the kitchen.

'Please tell your master,' she said, 'that it is *not* convenient to see him. Not convenient at all.'

She didn't even write it down.

CHAPTER ELEVEN

DEBBIE had once again made a fool of herself while doing her job, and this time it was Dr Oduloru who had saved her from her foolishness, with Jim as an observer, tight-lipped, standing by. She had been doing her job in a daze all day, and it so happened that one of her male patients, who had suffered an amputation for elephantiasis, was due to learn to walk on crutches, which the hospital carpenter had made to Debbie's requirements. She appeared with the crutches at four-thirty, telling the lad, who was about twenty-one, to get out of bed ready. Her assistant, Oliver, was standing by to learn how one helped a patient walk on crutches: the young man could already hop to and from the bathroom on his one good leg and was inclined to be a wag. Debbie said, 'Now lift up your arm——' and put a crutch beneath his armpit, ensuring that it was not too long and so force up his shoulders—'that seems fine,' she said, when suddenly the young man fell against her and she grabbed hold of him instinctively. Immediately the crutch fell to the floor and she was supporting his whole weight.

'Oliver!' she called. 'Help me!'

Oliver's idea of help was to pick up the crutch and meanwhile, from other beds, shouts of ribald laughter and obviously rude remarks rent the air. Debbie began to suspect what was happening when she looked up and saw the patient's dull brown eyes upon her lewdly; it was he who was holding on to her rather than the reverse, and she could smell his sweat, saw beads appearing on his brow and shouted 'Oliver!' again as his weight bore them both to the ground. Dr Oduloru's voice brought sanity to the ward immediately and the culprit was censured sharply and sent back to his bed. Debbie was summoned to Dr Oduloru's office, together with Jim, where she sat feeling miserable as nobody spoke.

'I'm making a mess of things, aren't I?' she asked at length. 'I'm very sorry, Dr Oduloru. I don't quite understand how that happened.'

'Oh, but I do, my dear Miss Wyndham. I know my people. I know how repressed young men are while saving up to afford a wife, which many of them can't do until they're in their thirties. I think it is I who should apologise to you for their behaviour.'

'I'm trying to train Oliver to deal with the men, but he's not up to it yet.'

'Of course not. You probably learned your skills at a college. If I had to level criticism it would be at Brant here——' Jim looked astounded—'for not telling me how pretty and nubile you were when he sang your praises to me originally. I think when you're working in the men's ward, in future, a member of the medical staff, or Sister, must be there to supervise. That will be all, Miss Wyndham. Don't worry about it.'

Outside in the corridor, Jim said, 'I don't know how you manage it, Debbie! I honestly don't. If you could have seen yourself rolling on the floor with that lout——'

'Oh, shut up!' Debbie suddenly flared. 'I've had

enough, without you starting. And I'm not going to the Club this evening. I have a headache.' She stalked off.

She walked down to her house later, feeling a failure in everything, her job, her love life, the lot. She groaned 'Oh, no!' as Marc stepped out of the shadows to confront her. 'What do *you* want?' she asked ungraciously.

'Well, I'm obviously not going to get it, if it was a little civilised conversation I was after.'

'I'm sorry. I'm tired, and I've been ill.'

'Yes, I know. Let me take you to my place for a quiet meal and you can relax.'

'I thought I'd already made it clear that we shouldn't meet?'

'It may be clear to you why we shouldn't, but not to me. I must be dense. Perhaps you'll come and explain so that even I can understand? I'm sorry to be a bore, but I'll have to have satisfaction from you before I'll give up trying. Come on! You needn't change.'

Debbie felt as though she was sinking into quicksand. If she took one step with him she was lost. She made a final effort by resurrecting what was left of her anger with Jim and fanning it.

'Can't you get it into your head that I'm not going anywhere with you? I've tried to make it clear that it's all over between us. I can't say it any plainer than that. Now leave me alone and go away!'

She hadn't been aware of the dog until that moment, but sensing that she spoke in anger against his master, Wolf growled in sudden menace.

Marc spoke to the dog sharply in French, and turned on his heel and left. Only when Debbie turned miserably to step into her little house did she see the dog still there, barring her way, showing every excellent tooth in his head.

'Kadiri!' she called urgently, and Wolf took a step towards her, holding one paw in mid-air like a pointer dog.

'Yes, missie?' asked the lad.

'Can you get rid of this animal? He frightens me.'

Kadiri approached and got the same threatening treatment.

'I not fight with that dog,' he said. 'I t'ink he want you do somet'ing. You better do. He once hunt t'ief who steal from Master Roland. Hunt him right back to Master Roland's house. Mebbe Missie have something Master Roland want?'

'No, I haven't, and I'm not going to be intimidated by a dog. Go home, Wolf!' She tried to be firm, but her voice wobbled and in the face of those shining teeth she wavered, but decided if she once got inside the house she could at least shut this menace out. Getting inside, however, wasn't easy, and as she tried to force her way past the dog he took her literally by the arm, gently, at this stage, but still grumbling in his throat to remind her that he wasn't joking.

'What do you want, Wolf?' she asked, trying to be reasonable. 'Tell me what you want. A nice bone?' she coaxed.

He released her arm and instead took a grip on her white overall and tugged.

'Where to?' she asked, and he tugged more as she took a step or two into the darkness, so that the material ripped.

'Damn!' she said, and spoke to Kadiri, who was still watching with interest. 'Give me a torch, please,' she said. 'If I've got to go to Mr Roland's I'm not going to be driven there like a sheep. I'll take the blessed dog home and give his master a piece of my mind!'

Thus it was that she faced Marc once again, breathing heavily and oozing the kind of hostility one reserves for those who are nearest and dearest. He, too, was obviously in an emotional state, and if they had so much as brushed fingers at that stage, then nature would have done the rest for them and in electrical fusion have healed the breach. Words, however, which are black and white things, as opposed to the blinding colours of emotions, succeeded in widening the gap between them.

'I suppose it was Wolf who tore your dress?'

'Well, what did you expect when I suppose you told him to deliver me dead or alive?'

'Now, don't exaggerate. He——'

'What do you mean, don't exaggerate? Am I here by my own will, or by yours? Aided and abetted by that brute out there, who ought to be put down. He's not safe to be around.'

'I'm sufficiently ashamed of my actions without you getting hysterical over Wolf. I didn't realise I was so hypersensitive. I just couldn't accept being dismissed like a recalcitrant steward-boy from your presence.'

'Well, now that I am here, what do you want me to say?'

'Surely what I want you to say isn't the point? I simply thought it cowardly of you to resort to letters and insulting verbal messages, via one of my stewards, regarding what to me, at least, was a vital issue. You won't join me in a meal?'

'I'd rather not. But I will have a long, cool drink,' she relented. 'I've had quite a walk, considering I don't feel very energetic yet.'

'Again, I'm sorry. I never did anything like that before. I never felt quite so harshly about a woman previously.'

Debbie tried not to look him in the face as she sipped the lime, just flavoured with lager, and with ice cooling it.

'Well, I'm here in person now, as you requested, and I repeat that I don't think we should see each other again.'

'Have I the right to an explanation of your apparent change of heart? I mean, I don't fall in love every day, and being kicked in the teeth for my pains isn't a thing I want to make a habit of.'

'Then you mustn't make a habit of choosing the wrong women.' At last she looked at him and wished she hadn't. The tears a man refuses to shed, when he is hurt, had somehow taken the brilliance from his eyes.

'Was it something I said or did, Debbie?' He was actually appealing to her and she couldn't bear it.

'Oh, lord, no!' she said quickly. 'It was just all wrong. I mean put two characters on a desert island and they'll think they're Mr and Miss Wonderful, and the rest-house was a bit like that. It's perhaps as well we got away. We were starting to make the play look like reality, but it really was just a play. We wrote the script as we went along and we mustn't forget we were only acting.'

He had himself outwardly under control again, and nodded as though feeling much wiser.

'Just assure me on one point. Sister Meadows hasn't been influencing you against me?'

'Not in the least,' she could answer quite honestly. 'Sister hasn't that sort of influence over me. I make my own decisions. I can only apologise if I appeared frivolous when I was with you.'

'Oh, you didn't appear frivolous, believe me! I couldn't have taken you more seriously. But I am learning that women are not necessarily what they say or how they behave. I will take that sobering thought on tour with me, because you see, tomorrow I start on my annual tour of the Central Eastern region, which is under my jurisdiction. I'll be away for eight weeks. I had even planned to pick up a parson en route to marry us on my return. Wasn't I a fool? It was the only thing which I thought would make this separation tolerable. Instead of which I'll be glad to get away, even with egg on my face, as I believe the Americans say.'

Debbie was shocked to hear he was going away, too, though she daren't show it. She said, 'You mustn't let this sort of thing put you off women. I mean, all girls aren't——' she almost choked—'aren't having you on. You just have to find the right one.' She had finished her drink and noticed he was smiling wryly. 'Now may I go?'

'Having me on,' he said, rising, 'is that what it was? You were having me on?'

Suddenly he swooped and, pinioning her arms, pressed harshly and cruelly on her protesting lips. It was only when she whimpered that he let her go and this time it was he who avoided her eyes.

It certainly was hot, though Debbie really didn't notice the weather much. Nigeria was invariably hot and degrees didn't concern her. One took salt tablets and drank a lot so that whatever one lost in perspiration the body retained sufficient fluid for its needs. Having the use of the jeep made her self-sufficient and she occasionally went to the Club for a meal or just to be in the thick of things, and one evening she saw Mary dining alone, who beckoned her to her table. She realised that Mary must be feeling lonely, too, though her long acquaintance with Marc must have familiarised her with this annual safari he made.

'Everything all right with you, Mary?' she asked, studying the menu and ordering a vegetable curry.

'Yes, fine, thanks. And you?'

'I haven't long to go now. I suppose I should be thinking about sending off my advance luggage and just keeping what I need.'

'Have you enjoyed being in Nigeria?'

'Curate's egg,' said Debbie. 'Of course there have been good parts. But professionally it's very restricting.'

They chatted of this and that, even of fashions, and then Mary said, 'I see Jim has just come in. Yoo-hoo! Jim!'

Debbie said, 'Oh, nothing personal, Jim, but I was just going. I want to finish a letter arranging about digs back home.'

'I shall take it very personally unless you let me buy you a drink first, Debbie.'

'Oh, O.K., then. A very little gin with a lot of lime, please.'

She looked at Jim as she sipped her drink. The warm soul of his eyes glowed as he laughed at something Mary was saying. Why couldn't she have remained in love with Jim? It had been so comfortable, never, perhaps, scaling the heights but never grovelling in the depths, either. But Jim and Debbie were history, now. One couldn't travel back into history.

'Now I must go,' she said at length, and nobody argued further. She heard Mary laughing light-heartedly as she crossed the dining-room, twinkled her fingers at Colonel and Mrs Thompson and went out into the night.

She was puttering away on a drum Kadiri had given her when Jim called to see her the following evening.

'Oh, so it's you making that row every night, is it?' he asked benignly. 'If you don't watch out you'll be getting Africa into your blood.'

'Help yourself to a drink,' Debbie said, putting the drum aside. 'There's nothing wrong, is there?'

'Why should anything be wrong?' asked Jim, trying to smile and grimacing instead. 'I come to see my ex-fiancée and she asks me what's wrong.'

Debbie looked at him in a studying way. 'Do you know that's the first time you've called me your ex-fiancée?' she asked.

'I know.' Jim suddenly looked nervous as he poured himself a sherry. 'That's what I've come about. Are you?'

'Am I what, Jim?' Debbie asked, as calmly as she could.

'My ex-fiancée. I mean, is it really all over between us, Debbie?'

'Well, I think so, Jim. I'd like you to think so, too. I

mean, you're a nice person and I wouldn't want to hurt you.'

'You said that of your own accord, didn't you, Debbie?' his hand trembled so that he spilt some sherry. 'I didn't make you say it by any action of mine?'

'No, you didn't. I say!' the light was beginning to dawn for Debbie—'I do believe there's someone else and oh, Jim, I am glad! I honestly am.'

'Are you, Debbie? Are you really? Can an ex-fiancé kiss you?'

Somehow their lips made contact, but it was like puppies playing. Jim was far too excited to concentrate.

'Would you come and tell her yourself that it's all over and nobody's hurt? She's been dining with me and somehow it was the right time to ask, and I know she loves me, but she wants to be sure you have nothing against it. I mean, she knows about us.'

'Of course I'll come and tell the lucky lady that she's all yours, and that I wish you both all the happiness in the world.'

Arm in arm, like tried old friends, they went past the tennis courts and across the compound and into Jim's bungalow. Debbie was about to say, 'Well, Sister, you'll never get your bedspread finished now,' when the words froze on her lips, for it was Mary who rose to meet her—Mary in the same old tussore dress, eyes like brilliants and smiling expectantly up at the other.

'Mary! It's you?'

'You don't approve?' Mary's countenance dimmed as though happiness could be blotted out.

'Of course I approve. I approve absolutely. It's just that—well, I'm amazed. You and Jim—I can't believe it!'

'But, Debbie,' Mary pleaded weakly, 'our little talk. You said, if you remember?'

'I remember everything I said, and do you know I thought we were talking about Jean-Marc Roland?'

'Marc's a dear, but he looks on me as a sister. Debbie, you really don't mind about me and Jim, do you?'

It was Jim who started to laugh, and Mary who joined in and then Debbie until the whole thing began to sound rather hysterical. Sister appeared in the doorway and smiled indulgently; she was busily crocheting as she stood.

'Well, you three seem to have successfully sorted yourselves out,' she observed. 'I don't know what to make of you. First it's Jack and Jill and then Jack gets somebody else.'

'Weren't Jack and Jill brother and sister?' asked Mary. Somehow this started the three laughing helplessly again. Sister, still smiling her calm, contented smile, slid off quietly into the night and left them to it.

The morning had been heavy, and the sky was leaden. Shortly after breakfast distant thunder could be heard.

'That means the rain has started up on the plateau,' Jim remarked to Debbie as they met on the women's ward. 'It could reach us today or tomorrow. Mary's fretting a bit about Marc Roland getting back. He could be stranded by flooding if he's not quick.'

Debbie's heart turned over as usual at the mention of Marc's name. She had not confided how she felt about him to either Jim or Mary, but sometimes she wondered if they suspected, as she had pumped the latter as to his whereabouts.

'Oh, he's headed for home by now,' Mary had said confidently, 'but how far away I wouldn't know. I almost sent him my news by the drums,' and she laughed, 'but then I thought that good news will always keep.'

'The drums?' Debbie asked.

'Oh, yes. If you can find a good drummer—and they're getting scarcer all the time—you can either send a message or receive one. But I'd rather like to see Marc's face when I tell him about Jim and me.'

Debbie thought about both Mary's and Jim's words all that day, thinking that if Marc did get stranded by floods then she might have to leave Nigeria without telling him of the ghastly mess she had made of things, and that she did love him and had always loved him. Even when she was falling over him on the plane and thinking she hated him, it was emotion strong enough to turn its coat and become love. Deep feelings of any kind about a member of the opposite sex are always significant: it is indifference which has no future.

That evening while thunder rolled and lightning lit up the evening sky, she said to Kadiri, 'Can you really say anything on the drums? I mean, are you as good a drummer as you say?'

'I best drummer in my village. My fader used to drum for tourists up Jos way. He teach me all he know. But when he die I have to work help family. I eldest son. But also I get money for drumming sometimes.'

'Could you find out where Master Roland is, Kadiri?'

'Oh, that I know already. Yesterday he was at Mataka, two days' travel away. I hear dat on drum last night.'

'Then he could be only one day's travel away now?'

Kadiri carefully put down the glass he was polishing after blowing on it.

'Missie want to know?' he asked. 'Missie got no animal need vet.'

'But I'm thinking of getting a kitten,' Debbie fibbed, 'and I'd like to know where he is—Master Roland, I mean.'

'Missie go back England in two weeks and get kitten now?' Kadiri asked disbelievingly. 'Oh, missie, I t'ink you pull Kadiri in the leg.' She had taught him this expression, but he always said it in his own quaint way.

'Oh, Kadiri, I want to get a message to Master Roland. If you can speak so well on the drums, please help me!'

'You come my village one hour,' he told her, 'when I finish all job. O.K.?'

'O.K.,' she told him, and tried not to wonder if Marc had succeeded in putting her out of his mind these intervening weeks. She couldn't blame him if he had. She had humiliated him and made their parting, and her decision, sound so very final.

The people of Kadiri's village had accepted her appearances among them by now. She was always treated as an honoured guest and sat among the women, though on an old deck-chair which they produced for her, whereas they sat on the ground. Dina was helping older girls cook over an open fire and Debbie was the first to be served with a kind of kebab, which was delicious.

Kadiri came over from the men's side, his slight but well-muscled body bare except for his lion cloth, and asked her what he was to say on the drums.

'Find out where Master Roland is first, Kadiri.'

He came back to say that Master Roland's party was staying in the Ete Moto rest-house for the night. 'What I say now?' he asked.

'Could you tell him I love him?' Debbie asked above a thunder crash which made some of the younger children whimper and crowd round their mothers.

'How I say dat?'

'Just say "I love you". That's all. He'll understand.'

'But I talking to man in Ete Moto village. If I say "I love you", all girl t'ink I love dem. I no go for marry long time yet. I no get money for bride-price.'

'Kadiri, say you have a message for Master Roland, and then say "She loves you". Please try.'

'I go for look big fool,' Kadiri grumbled, going back to the male lines.

As he drummed, some of the older men, who understood every nuance of the drumming, began to smile and then to laugh openly. They told those who didn't understand and finally the girls and women were shaking with laughter. Kadiri hung his head when he had finished and Debbie wondered if she had strained their relationship too much, but when distant drums throbbed over the heavy air the boy hushed the rest and just listened. A slow smile broke over his dusky countenance and his excellent teeth gleamed in the firelight.

'Master Roland say he go for love you too, missie,' he called across the open space, 'and he home tomorrow.'

Everybody hearing this and understanding, or having it interpreted for them, began to laugh again, but they laughed approvingly and raised their hands or cups towards their guest, for it is said that all the world loves a lover, and Africa is no exception.

Debbie, who had risen to her feet when Kadiri addressed her, now sank down, feeling peculiarly weak, into her chair, but this was now too rickety to support her and she found herself falling into the long grass which surrounded the clearing. It was at that moment a snake, thinking the outstretched white arm was about to attack it, struck.

Debbie swam to the surface and recoiled from the sight of a green reptile nailed to the wall at her side.

'Hello!' Jim greeted. 'That's the blighter that bit you. Fortunately not too poisonous, but it can be very painful. Your boy turned surgeon, cut your arm and sucked the worst of the venom out, but I thought after I'd fixed a dressing I'd better put you out for the night. For the night, did I say? It's two in the afternoon.'

'Oh, Jim! Your siesta time.'

'Don't worry about that, old girl. I'm just glad it wasn't a krite got you. You'll have a sore arm for a day or two, but nothing worse. Right, I'll love you and leave you.'

Debbie somehow managed to dress herself, but Kadiri came in, fussily, when he heard her moving and, without self-consciousness, fastened her buttons and zips before examining her appearance.

'You go for look nice,' he said approvingly, and she half staggered into her living-room. She looked un-comprehendingly up at the tall figure waiting to see her, and tried to swallow something like a tennis ball which had formed in her throat.

'One more shock like that might be fatal,' said her visitor wryly.

'Oh, Marc!' She hurled herself upon him and then the lump dissolved and poured out as tears from her eyes, so that she soaked the front of his shirt and still found more to shed.

'Hey, hey!' he said at length. 'It rained all night, you know. You don't need to help the water situation.'

Her tears turned to laughter, and in a moment he had swept her up into his arms and carried her off outdoors.

'I *can* walk,' she said, keeping her cheek close to his, nevertheless. 'I was bitten in the arm, my legs are O.K.'

'Don't rob me of my simple pleasures,' he told her, stooping to kiss her lips lightly to the delight of patients occupying the wide verandas facing on to the compound. 'I take it you're excused duty?' he asked as he put her into the passenger seat of his car. 'Otherwise it's too bad.'

'I was in my last fortnight,' Debbie assured him, 'and what I remember of last night is Dr Oduloru saying I hadn't to worry about working but to make the rest of my time here a holiday.'

'Could you manage a honeymoon?' Marc asked.

There was so much to say, and so much to do and so much to feel. Explanations were really unimportant, but they were made, and so involved were these two that they didn't notice the rain pouring down outside and the sun coming out and turning the compound outside Marc's bungalow into a steam-bath, and then the dramatic sunset against the purple of stormclouds, and Festus serving the meal in a plastic pixie-hood, which he had forgotten to remove along with his mac in his dash across the compound.

There was more and more to talk about, to discuss, and plan. An early wedding, with relatives and friends told afterwards.

'I'm not letting you out of my sight again,' Marc said darkly. 'I've had seven and a half weeks of hell. I'm due for leave in June, when we can visit your folk and mine, though, of course, anybody's welcome to come out and see us in the meanwhile.'

Oh, what joyful matters to speak of!

Oh, what togetherness was wrought in these two.

A third presence finally would be ignored no longer. Wolf, who had come inside, insinuated his hairy presence between them. He nuzzled Debbie away first, and then his master.

'I'd forgotten you, boy,' said Marc, with a deep sigh. 'Walkie, eh? You coming, Debbie?'

'I wouldn't miss it.'

He put his college scarf round her neck and used it to draw her towards him. Wolf barked warningly, that matters with him were urgent, and all three went down the veranda steps. They walked idly, still with so much to say, and so much to dally over, while Wolf shot here and there in the darkness, favouring a particular tree here, chasing a flying squirrel there, and then Debbie paused to remark, 'That scent—it's not jasmine, is it?'

Everything had a smell after the rain, the earth, the wet, refreshed leaves, frangipani and orange blossom, but Marc suddenly sniffed like a hunting dog and looked up to where the moon, large and whole like an unchipped plate, suddenly appeared in a gap in the clouds.

'I wonder?' he questioned, and taking Debbie's hand

began to run. They arrived out of breath in the bare circle where they had lingered that first walk of theirs, only suddenly it wasn't bare. White petals were opening like miniature umbrellas wherever they looked, and the scent they exuded was almost breathtaking. The speed with which the blooms unfolded had to be seen to be believed, and while the sweethearts watched, enchanted, the whole glade became an arena of concentrated sweetness, a fairy ballet performed by nature for only one command performance in the year.

'At last I've seen it,' said Marc, almost reverently. 'The night of the moonflowers, and as if that wasn't almost unbelievable, I've got you too, my darling!'

'Only I won't go away,' Debbie said as they kissed, 'except with you. I'm not going to be a moonflower, Marc, I'm going to be a burr. Do you mind?'

'Start now,' he said contentedly, drawing her down to the soft, damp turf. 'Just cling.'

The flowers breathed their short lives away in a kind of ecstasy, the prowling dog, feeling sympathy with his lupine ancestors, howled at the moon and perhaps wondered at the eccentricities of human behaviour, and far away the thunder rolled over the high plateau, leaving only the tropical night, and silence.

<u>Two</u> more Doctor Nurse Romances to look out for this month

Mills & Boon Doctor Nurse Romances are proving very popular indeed. Stories range wide throughout the world of medicine – from high-technology modern hospitals to the lonely life of a nurse in a small rural community.
These are the other two titles for October.

DOCTORS IN SHADOW
by Sonia Deane

When Nurse Emma Reade comes to look after Dr Simon Conway's mother and help in his practice, she realises it will be impossible to live in the same house with such a man and not fall in love. But one of the other doctors, Odile Craig, adores him – and is fiercely possessive . . .

BRIGHT CRYSTALS
by Lilian Darcy

In the French Alps Nurse Natalie Perroux meets a handsome member of the ski rescue team – and they are instantly attracted. What she doesn't foresee is the heart-rending tangle which follows the unexpected arrival of an old boyfriend from England . . .

On sale where you buy Mills & Boon romances

The Mills & Boon rose is the rose of romance

Look out for these three great Doctor Nurse Romances coming next month

THE DOCTOR'S DECISION
by Elizabeth Petty

When Staff-Nurse Anna Forster meets the new Senior Surgical Registrar at the Calderbury Royal she realises that most clouds *do* have a silver lining. It is love at first sight for Anna, but is it the same for Paul Keslar?

A BRIDE FOR THE SURGEON
by Hazel Fielding

By marrying Pip, Hallam Fielding would gain a clinic nurse, a general secretary, cook, housekeeper and slave – and all for free! Even if he could never love her, was it sufficient if she could somehow make him want her?

NURSE RHONA'S ROMANCE
by Anne Vinton

Rhona was disappointed, though not heartbroken, when her romance with Chris Willson came to nothing: all the same, she was glad to have her work as a district nurse to take her mind off things. And she was even more thankful for her career when her next romance, with Dr Alex Denham, crashed to disaster.

On sale where you buy Mills & Boon romances.

The Mills & Boon rose is the rose of romance

'Everyone loves romance
at Christmas'

The Mills & Boon Christmas Gift Pack is available
from October 9th in the U.K. It contains four new
paperback Romances from four favourite authors,
in an attractive presentation case:

The Silken Cage	– Rebecca Stratton
Egyptian Honeymoon	– Elizabeth Ashton
Dangerous	– Charlotte Lamb
Freedom to Love	– Carole Mortimer

You do not pay any extra for the pack – so put it on
your Christmas shopping list now.
On sale where you buy paperbacks, £3.00 (U.K. net).

The rose of romance
Mills & Boon